RN

OUT OF WORK

OUT
OF
WORK

Stories and novella

GREG MULCAHY

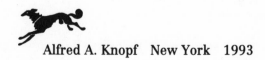

Alfred A. Knopf   New York   1993

THIS IS A BORZOI BOOK
PUBLISHED BY ALFRED A. KNOPF, INC.

COPYRIGHT © 1993 BY GREG MULCAHY

A PORTION OF "A HISTORY OF AMNESIA" APPEARED IN *CALI-
BAN*. "SEASONAL" APPEARED, IN DIFFERENT FORM AND
WITH A DIFFERENT TITLE, IN *MISSISSIPPI MUD*. MOST OF THE
OTHER FICTIONS IN THIS BOOK WERE PUBLISHED IN *THE
QUARTERLY*.

LIBRARY OF CONGRESS CATALOGING-IN-PUBLICATION DATA
MULCAHY, GREG.
    OUT OF WORK : STORIES / BY GREG MULCAHY. — 1ST ED.
     P. CM.
    ISBN 0-679-41967-5
    I. TITLE.
    PS3563.U389O94 1993
    813'.54 — DC20   92-54799
                                       CIP

MANUFACTURED IN THE UNITED STATES OF AMERICA
FIRST EDITION

THIS BOOK IS FOR ABIGAIL AND HER CHILDREN —

AND FOR TRUE BELIEVER GORDON LISH

CONTENTS

OUT OF WORK

$$$$

A message on the door. He knew about those. Throughout history, famous messages recorded for all to see. This, what was this? A bit of green paper rc'ied scroll-like and jammed beneath the crooked handle of the storm door. Message — more of a flier, really. Not targeted to anyone in particular. Targeted to a class — say, people who ordered pizza, or home psychotherapy, or needed their gutters cleaned.

So he took this flier, limp with fog, and spread it flat on the dining room table:

FOOD

$$$$

****

SAVE 80% OFF RETAIL

and a phone number. There was more on the back, the explanation. What you paid, how much you saved, and a sample menu of the staples you received each month for your fee.

He looked at the menu and roughed out the math. Seemed like a pretty good deal, maybe not as big a savings as claimed, but a savings. The problem was the menu's vagueness. It said *pasta*. What did *pasta* mean? He would get a pound. If he got fettuccine or lasagna, he would be happy, but he did not eat asini de pepe or vermicelli, and

3

what if they gave him shells? What on earth would he do with a pound of shells?

He never thought he would be in for this.

Not this, exactly, but things like this. He had known people who were involved in things like this.

Not him. Maybe some people at work, when he had had the job, some of the staff people, or some distant relatives, third cousins who had not done too well in life.

He had lost the house, Jesus bloody Christ, could he go a day without remembering he had lost the house? And now this, this was on his door.

Food. What could he say to that?

He showed his wife the flier.

"I don't know," she said.

He did the shopping. That was only fair, with her working most of the time. And he was good at it; he had thought about it, studied it, learned it down to a science. He could, with ease, get nourishing food for the family for thirty dollars a week. Under thirty dollars a week. He could easily provide well-balanced meals at this discount price if only they would listen. If only they would stop these special requests—the shampoos, complexion soaps, snack treats—all these things he could get at the discount store—if not the brands they wanted, something similar, almost the same, the same goddamned thing except for the fucking four-color package—all these things, if only they would be patient, and accept the off-brands, and get them at the discount store instead of the grocery store where the markup was what—two hundred percent?

"It may be a good idea," his wife said. "But what do you think the kids will think?"

He did not say what the kids might think.

"You know," she said, "how kids are."

He hated to think about it. But he knew. And these were his kids. Did they not deserve something more than what they had? Kids, after all, were only kids once. Should he visit his problems upon them?

Would they eat chicken hot dogs?

And if they would eat them now, they would not eat them forever. Kids got that age, that certain age when they decided nothing was good enough. Nothing but the best then. Not just food, they would want the best clothes as well. Designer brands.

And, of course, the house. Not only would they continue to refer to the lost house, the house which, in fact, had not been much of a house anyway, thirty or so years old, cheaply prefabricated, worked over by three generations of inept do-it-yourselfer owners, the house they had all bitched about then, but now remembered and transformed, in their minds, from a minimal tract unit to the lost seat of family honor, not only would they refer to that house, but they would be ashamed of their current dwelling, even if it were not this shabby rental, even if it were a mansion, they would be forever ashamed and their shame would be forever directed at him, the ongoing indictment of his life.

He knew.

His children would never forgive him.

Maybe he needed something like the food club. That was what his wife told him. He was standing in the kitchen, filling an on-the-rocks glass with gin, and she said, "Maybe you need this."

He was not so stupid as to say anything.

As to rise to the bait.

He took a long drink.

She looked him steadily in the eye.

He raised his glass. "To the ghosts of the past."

What he needed, yes, what he needed was the food club. Or something like it. He needed to get something going. He had a little thing, a few hours a day, but it was not enough, and he had to face the reality that it would never be enough. Other people had networks—hustled three or four things, cosmetics, laundry soap, telemarketing, office cleaning, newspaper delivery—put these things in combination, and they did all right. Sure, they worked hard. That, and they saved. Every penny. Then, they got into something—little business of their own—and they were okay.

Their lives were not perfect, but they had some control.

If he could join the club and turn it to his advantage. Really make something of it.

It was what he needed.

The club was a cinderblock warehouse on a dirt lot surrounded by a cyclone fence. The fence was topped with razor wire. He drove through the main gates. It had rained earlier in the week, and the lot was crisscrossed with muddy ruts. Rusting pieces of metal were scattered around. He remembered that this place had once been a truck parts lot.

He tried to remember what it had been called.

Now there was a sign, a plastic banner secured to the cinderblock, that read FOOD CLUB.

FOOD CLUB in black letters on the white vinyl.

Everything, he thought, is just what it is.

He often thought this.

It gave him a kind of comfort.

He stood in a long line, flier in hand. Those without fliers were sent away.

The man at the table took the flier and punched his name and address into a computer terminal.

"Yup," the man said, "you're eligible."

He nodded. Smiled. Why not? Eligible. Inside.

"You understand," the man said, "you have to work ten hours a week?"

"Work?" he said.

"It's like a co-op."

"It is, is it?" He nodded. Ten hours a week. What was his time worth?

Plus the drive.

He stood looking at the man and the computer and the racks of food, the warehouse of staples, and he understood, at last, the temptation to go, to disappear as gone as his house was gone.

The man had a form for him to sign.

And he knew he would stay, and sign the form, and join the club.

Maybe there would be a club meeting, once a year, a picnic, and the members and their wives and children would gather at the strip of city park beside the dismal river and build fires in the rusting municipally owned grills and eat chicken hot dogs and beans and welfare cheese and drink generic beer in a spirit of fellowship, of good will, of community.

Lesson

The teacher has a boot knife with a rubberized handle. He is showing it around. Somebody says, "The handle is made of rubber." "The handle," the teacher says, "is not made of rubber. It is rubberized." The teacher spells out the word. "All of the best equipment, the truly professional stuff, was rubberized at one time," the teacher says. "Completely nonporous," the teacher says, "nothing could penetrate." "Not much of a blade," the teacher says, "but for the point. It could leave a nasty puncture." The teacher puts the boot knife in his boot.

He works out of a boarded-up storefront in a neighborhood of old buildings: houses, apartments, service stations. There are not many businesses left in the neighborhood. The teacher's operation is not, conventionally speaking, a business.

The teacher has a stacked deck. In addition to the boot knife, there is a stacked deck. No one has ever seen it, but the teacher has it. He says so. "Rest assured I have it," he says if he is asked to display it. The teacher does not refuse to display the stacked deck, not in so many words. He jerks his head toward the locked steel door at the back of the room. The words STORE ROOM are stencilled on the door. The teacher dangles his ring of keys and says, "Plenty more where this came from."

Lest anyone become agitated, the teacher is quick to reassure. He uses only officially issued equipment. Although his is a private concern and not bound by general regulation, let there be no doubt all is scrutinized by the appropriate governing body and all comes through fully approved. For your protection. There is even—as the teacher is well aware, though you may not be—some talk. Some growing concern. Some movement toward legislation. The teacher is neither opposed nor supportive. He sees the situation objectively. He listens to the arguments, his teacher's mind separating emotion from reason, discerning the elegant lines of pure logic stripped bare of feeling, social baggage, class and gender bias. The teacher sees both sides and remains impartial. Detached. In any case, the teacher is secure in the knowledge that legislation will have no effect upon him. The teacher pre-exists the law.

The teacher rejects the easy answers, the easy definitions, the easy platitudes. Unless. Unless they serve as a starting point. A launching pad. A place to begin. Or. They can be turned somehow to the teacher's ends. For example. "If," the teacher says, "everything goes up in flame and light, why are you here?" He looks slowly around the storefront, catching each student's eyes with his own. Holding them. Not for long. But it seems longer. It is part of his, the teacher's, routine. It makes them more aware. For a moment.

Perhaps, the teacher allows, he has framed the question incorrectly. "Perhaps," the teacher says, "I need to make a statement." The students pick up their pens, smooth their notebook pages. "When," the teacher says, "you abided in bliss, you had no need of knowledge." The students write.

There are slides. Boxed, most of them. Some might still be in the plastic carousel. In the store room.

The teacher has cabinets full of things.
In the store room.
Jars and bottles.
Pickled specimens.
Wrinkled organs.

Floodlight

He left town right after high school.

Then he went home and got on at the plant. After a few months he knew he did not want to be an idiot in a bump cap for the rest of his life. The high-school principal, an old schoolmate, got his certification waived, and he started teaching. At first he tried too hard; then he eased up.

The kids were not bad. They made a time line that ran around the room, beneath the pictures of dead presidents. He told them about the shift from hunting to agriculture.

The women he had known were mostly gone. Sometimes he went out with a woman from the next town, a fellow teacher. He lived in a bungalow on the edge of town. The house was small and neat, with a yard that gave way to woods. A floodlight was mounted over the back steps, and there were iron clothespoles like equidistant crosses in the yard.

Sometimes he would run into a success story back for a class reunion.

He could not blame the graduates for leaving.

Seemed like a prank when the trouble started.

Someone got him on the mailing list of a firm that sold sex toys. The illustrated catalog arrived for him at school.

Somebody slashed a tire on his car.

Put a rock through a window of his house.

Took a case of Schmidt that was cooling on the back

steps one Saturday night. He had not heard a thing. He got a new bulb for the floodlight. Put out another case and waited in the dark house until he fell asleep in his chair. One afternoon the beer was gone.

His uncle had left a single-barreled shotgun and a coffee can of shells on a shelf in the basement. He went to the sporting-goods store to get a gun-cleaning kit. In the boating department, he found some 12-gauge flares. The man said they could be fired from a shotgun or a special launcher.

He had the window open about four inches. He practiced moving the barrel around in the frame.

He heard something late. Labored breathing. He was not sure it was not his own. He heard something out there on the concrete steps. He shoved the barrel out the window and fired.

The flare blinded him.

Everything smelled burnt.

A man was out there. His foot was caught on the bottom step.

One of the transients from the railroad tracks, the sheriff said. Sometimes they came up to town.

His lawyer told him to keep his mouth shut. He did. The grand jury did not return a bill, and he was free of legal entanglements.

He lost interest in the work. Resigned.

At night he sat at the kitchen door, drinking.

Days, he filled his big green watering jug, wandered among the stones, putting water in the vases and in the cans of flowers.

Buy Out

Best job of my life, for a company that made lawnmowers. A multinational bought it out; I didn't make the cut. Piece of luck, the post office was giving tests. I got as far as the steps of the Federal Building; couldn't go through with it.

Was in the Midwest. My ex-wife was out East. I had a '79 Buick with ninety-seven thousand on it. Thought I'd go for a little visit. Packed what fit in the car, gave everything else away.

Got all the money I had. Five hundred in cash, twenty-eight hundred in fifty-dollar traveler's checks. I'd had twenty thousand once, but this was all that was left. Thought maybe I'd buy a house when I'd had the money. It didn't work out.

There was really no point in calling her. Not from so far away. Didn't want her to have too much notice. Wait till I was almost there, then let her know.

Drive was interesting at first. Saw a tornado. Green sky, black funnel, the whole thing. Heard sirens, saw a motel without a roof, cars on fire, trashed houses, fire trucks, ambulances.

Couple of states away, heard on the radio there were ten dead and seventeen injured. Stopped at a city in the mountains. Whole town looked like a slum. Motel was the usual set-up with a waffle and beer place for a restaurant. Wasn't as bad as you'd think.

. . .

Woke up in the middle of the night. Two guys in my
room. One had a big revolver. Other had a small automatic. They wanted my wallet. Revolver man took the
cash and threw the wallet to me. I was still in bed. It
landed on my chest. They didn't ask about anything else.
I didn't mention the traveler's checks in my bag. Automatic man told me to be quiet for a while after they left.
Said I would. Police said wasn't much they could do.

After a few hundred miles, I decided to turn off for
lunch. Was looking for a place, but there wasn't anything for a long way. Started to see signs for the thermal
spring. They looked kind of old, painted wood, but I
figured the owner wouldn't replace them if they were
still good enough to draw business. The signs told you
about the usual things—fireworks, gas, food, miniature
golf. Seemed to be spaced every two miles or so. Saw
the Thermal Springs This Exit sign and turned off.

Exit ramp was a long twist down a gully. Gully was
wooded. Road came to a rise, also wooded. It led down
another gully, then curved to the side. Stayed on it for a
mile. Blacktop ended, but the road kept on, a graveled
one-and-a-half lane. Looked for a wide spot. There wasn't
any. Road went up and around a mountain. Unfenced
edge gave way to a sheer drop. Stayed as close to the
inside as I could and crept up. Engine seemed to be
straining. Was getting to the top. Lights started going on
on the dash. I pushed it to the top. Level space that looked
long enough, then the steep graveled descent. The car
wasn't moving—locked up dead.

Popped the hood and got out. Radiator was steaming
and some belts were smoking. Touched the radiator cap

and yanked my hand away. Looked in the car. All the warning lights were on—hot, oil, alternator. Engine was making a weak whooshing sound. Shut it down and waited, wondering how this would turn out.

After about an hour, tried the radiator cap again. Wrapped my hand with a T-shirt first. It was still hot, but I got it off. Radiator empty, bone-dry. Looked around, down the mountain. Hoping for water—a stream, a puddle. Heard you could piss in a radiator in an emergency, didn't think I could fill it up.

Leaned against the door and tried to think. Later, I heard a car. Watched for it. White sedan, couldn't tell the make. When it got to the top, it stopped behind me and two men got out. They were wearing synthetic blue business suits. Thought they were salesmen.

You're blocking us, one said.

Little breakdown, the other said.

I told them I was glad to see them and asked for coolant or water or any liquid.

Don't have it, one said.

Can't help you, the other said.

Not with your car blocking us, the first said.

He went around to the back of the sedan and opened up the trunk.

Car's got to go, the second one said.

First one took a shotgun out of the trunk. Slammed the trunk shut, stepped around the car, shouldered the gun, and blew the driver's side window out of my car.

It's loaded, he said.

Sure is, the second one said.

He took a small automatic out of his pocket. Gun looked like the one the guy in the motel had. Stared at it.

Couldn't stop. Gunman pulled my suitcases out of my car.

Empty your pockets and put the stuff on the hood, the first one said.

Did it fast. Second one opened the driver's door of my car. Get in, he said. I sat behind the wheel. He leaned on the open door. The automatic was pointed at my head.

Foot on the brake, he said.

I nodded.

Put her in neutral, he said. Hands on the wheel.

Ready, the first one said.

Just about, the second one said. He reached into the car and put the muzzle of the pistol on my kneecap. Fired. I almost threw up. He got the other knee. I fainted for a second. Then I was steering as the car rolled down the road. Fainted again.

Don't know who brought me in. Woke up in the emergency room, spent a few weeks in the hospital. Orthoscope and all of it. Therapist told me I'd walk, but never the same. Other than the knees, there were a few gashes on my face from the broken windshield. The night nurse told me I was probably still delirious.

You kept talking about money and fish.

They gave me some metal canes with wrist cups on the ends of them. Got my traveler's checks replaced. Hospital got most of it. Gave me an itemized bill. Canes came to more than you'd think. Didn't know where to go. Walked out the double doors. There wasn't a cab stand. Receptionist in the lobby called for me. Driver explained that the hospital was a recent development, a for-profit operation a group of Asian investors ran from Manila or someplace. They built outside town to get the freeway accident trade. The town had been a coal railhead, then it was almost dead, but now there was work at the treatment plant. Asked what the plant treated. Driver said the feds built it for storage.

Dropped me at the only motel. It had been a franchise, but it had lost its affiliation. The chain's logo was painted over. Piled all the loose furniture behind the door and counted my money. Two hundred thirty-seven. No car.

Work was okay. Not as bad as you've been led to believe. Impressive facility. Technology's completely up to date. My job involved some caution, not too much skill. Monitor the situation, monitor the board, add necessary coolants—that kind of thing. At night, before I left the plant, go through all of the other monitors. Always tested out fine. Always wore all my safety equipment and checked my badge hourly.

Found an efficiency over an empty storefront in the empty downtown. Read the free papers from the supermarket rack. Federal money was floating around. The apartment was okay. Old fixtures, old paint, low rent. Everything worked.

Money wasn't bad. Food was high, but you accept that. Everything had to be trucked in. Otherwise the only expense was the therapy. Dropped it after four sessions. Wasn't doing any good. Bill, the foreman, sold me a Pinto for three hundred. Wasn't much, but it ran. For the groceries and that.

Had surplus income and my free time. Weekends and the off-hours. Naturally, I got to thinking. No point in calling my ex-wife. But I kept my eyes open.

A big glass case of pistols. I looked at the revolvers.

I want one, I told the clerk.

Single or double action?

What's the difference?

Single action, you cock the hammer every shot. You know, like a cowboy.

I want the kind you just pull the trigger, like on TV.

We talked caliber.

It's winter now, dark when I finish. See the lights of the facility in my rearview mirror. Stop at the drive-thru windows. One for food in styrofoam. Next for draft in styrofoam. Downtown's always empty.

My routine.

Orderly.

I sit by the window, aiming out.

This Is It

ometimes he would watch the news and not know what to think. He said, "I made it, and these other people did not." Perhaps it was all genetic. Other times he rejected the idea that people were wound to attain or to self-destruct. He would shake his head. The television was not that great, for that matter. What did it know?

He heard the joke about the president on his television. He told the joke to his wife the next morning. He went to work and told the joke to the fellows there. Scruffy-looking young people came to the house to canvass for the environment. He did not give them any money, but he told them the joke. At the mall, he got the door for a man carrying a box. They had a good laugh over the joke.

He went out on the walk and looked hard at the steps and porch. Sometimes people marked houses. Something on the door or a bent stem in the flower bed—anything they could see when they came back later for what they wanted. They knew the code and they had you down, assigned, figured as a member of a certain population, a recognizable subset. He hoped to find the mark and obliterate it before anyone got to him.

"How much sick time do you have coming?" his wife said.
    She thought they should get out of town for a while. It

was his fault that she felt this way. She had surprised him in the kitchen one morning while he was pounding it. He realized it was not good for her to see this.

"All you do," she said, "is make me sick."

She thought they would do well to rent a cabin in the North. The cabin came with a boat. The cabin had a fully equipped kitchen and knotty-pine paneling. It sat on a lake in a chain of lakes.

He had worked for years and this was the thanks he got. This and the possibility someone had marked his house and would be around as soon as he was gone.

"Those fish," he said, "stare at you."

His wife closed the curtains.

By then the boss was on him as well, telling him his performance was slipping, that he needed to take some time. The company had a new policy. They were encouraging people to get out, recharge. The rumor was accrual was on its way out; soon everyone would be forced to take his time or lose it.

He had his own ideas. The carpeting. The fibers emitted toxic materials. And the air-conditioning system was suspect. Who knew what organisms bred in the condensers? He could have thrown that in the boss's face, but he had no hard evidence.

The pressure was too much for him. He buckled.

He found a bump on his scrotum. He felt the bump, rolled it around in his fingers. This was, perhaps, what he had been waiting for. He felt sick and frightened. He had expected the heart or lungs or liver to go first. Some mornings he could feel them going as he stood in front of the mirror. And now this.

He squeezed the bump.

When he buckled, his boss said, "That's it."

There was no reason for his wife to know. What did she think? That he would sit home with the television, the table, the plates, the household cleaners? She would never understand the office was not his real work.

He went in at 4:00 a.m., and left after everyone else. The door stayed locked and the blinds stayed down. No lights. He told his wife he was on a special project.

He lit a cigarette. "They're giving me the nudge. The kiss of death is soon to follow." He felt the bump. He wondered who to call. Maybe he could get an implant.

He sat at the kitchen table.

His wife came in wearing her white nightgown. "Why are you here?" she said.

He cocked his head to one side and stared at her.

"Don't start anything," she said.

He just stared.

"What are you trying to pull?" she said.

Glass

I

Eddie Niijls' landlord comes by and says the building is being sold, and anyone not out by the end of the month will be evicted.

Eddie looks at his landlord's tie. All small dots.

—I know this is a hardship.

—I thought they gave you a tax break, Eddie says.

—Right, Ed, gave. Public-private partnership, place for the arts, they ran us all around the track.

—I thought—

—We had hopes, and we got shit. Privatization is the coming thing. They brought it down. I've got to live.

Eddie's dealer, George, calls and tells Eddie to stop by the gallery. Eddie considers his situation. He has, maybe, eight hundred bucks. A beautiful day. He watches a woman on a bicycle. She wears a spandex suit. Panels of color on the black. Fall season: geometrics. Bright rectangles. Mondrian.

Spray paint on a garage wall. X'd out. Triangles? Stars? Symbols.

Work in the streets. Guys started that way. Subways.

Eddie sees a bronze in the gallery. Three fused triangles. Smallest to largest. The largest eleven inches by eleven inches by eleven inches.

Like a miniature public piece.

Clean in a way.

Eddie does not recognize the artist's name.

Triangles.

—You are not moving forward, George says.

—So you dump me?

—A painter stalls, then comes back stronger.

—Come over and see what I'm doing.

George says he will be over in a few days.

Eddie calls around to see if anybody knows of a building with spacious flats that belongs to a widow who has not raised the rent in the years since her husband's death. Eddie's friends have heard of the place, but they are not sure where it is.

He needs to work. He has seventeen days. People move all the time.

Eddie goes into the spare room. His studio. No skylight, but there is a glass balcony door and a row of windows. As good light as can be got. Eddie takes a two-foot-by-two-foot sheet of quarter-inch plywood from the stack on the floor, sets it on the sawhorse table, and gives it a coat of cheap house paint. He does another. Another.

George says he will come around 3:00. Eddie cleans the place up. He sets the painting up in the spare room, then moves it to the living room. He puts the picture on a straight chair and places the desk lamp on the floor so its light shines on the canvas. He would like to hang the piece. That might be too much. George sees work rough every day.

Eddie has espresso, Chinese beer, wine. George is late. Eddie walks in circles.

George enters apologizing.

—You want a beer or something?

—Thanks, no time. Let's work.

Eddie motions toward the light. —The first in a series. Aluminum gray background. The words:

FEAR   BRAZIL

DESIRE BERLIN

DEATH   TAHITI

arranged in block letters.

—It is over, George says. Finished.

—But—

—Too concept. Too done.

—Uh—

—Maybe ten years ago. Maybe.

—Well—

—Now it's the sex thing. Get on board.

—Sex?

—Bodies. Or at least shapes. Curves, for Christ's sake.

Eddie cannot afford the same square footage. Not anywhere. He checks the want ads. Looks at a side-by-side duplex. Busted-up picket fence. Plywood over the basement windows. Thanks, no. Bodies. Curves. Ragged line of spray paint on the dirty wall. Break it up. Juxtaposed vertical lines. UPC.

I I

They come in a blast. Eddie crouches, hands before his face. The sun bright. Spandexed figures part as they fly past on roller blades.

—Bicycle trail, one yells.

Eddie sees the pictograph sign, moves from the tarmac to the sidewalk. Lake and ribbon of dirty sand—the nominal beach—to his right. By the waters of Calhoun. He steps around a thin young man who is carrying a cane. That back?

Look. Light breaking through the trees. Sail boats and sail boards contending on the water, neat triangles above fiberglass bases. A few fluffy clouds. Runners pass. Bronze flesh. Health.

Harps hanging in the trees. The angel of the Lord appears in the raiment of fire and glory to divide the multitudes—swimmers from sailors, skaters from joggers, sick from healthy—and dispense the awesome justice of the divine.

In the raiment of pure light.

Beer bottle. Clear. Mexican. Our friend glass.

He gets home. Number 103. The constant pressure of money. A fifteen-by-fifteen-foot efficiency with kitchenette and midget bath. Somebody painted the wooden floor. Scarred now. Canvas tacked to the sawhorse table. Only two windows. Hundred-watt bulbs in every fixture and three trouble lights hanging from nails.

Footsteps. The postman lugs his bag of despair.

Nothing falls through the slot.

Perhaps tomorrow.

Three hours till he has to be at work.

The supervisor bought his story. —Returning student, okay. Waxing experience?

He has floors six and eight. Office cleaning. Nice to

look at the individual touches in the cubicles. Calendars. Mugs. Cartoons.

Twenty hours a week. Covers the groceries and electric bill. With his savings.

Among the women at work, a woman. Eddie is taken by her hair. By her face. Body. Presence. Dolores. She has her story.

Eddie has trouble sleeping. And eating. Thinking. The future plays out before him.

Four-wheel drive in the parking lot. Chief Cherokee. Decorative strip on the side. Navaho pattern.

Kid from the janitorial service walks up. —Need something?

—I like the design.

The kid has a crinkly scar like a vaccination mark on his cheek.

He points to it. —A guy shot me.

He holds up his hand. Another scar. —Here too.

—Got to roll, Eddie says. See you.

A man with a video camera takes Eddie's picture.

He tries stencils. Repeated patterns. The alphabet.

George looks fit.

—Lose some weight?

—No, no. I'm on a new program.

—Seems to be working for you.

—I think so; perhaps I flatter myself.

．　．　．

The ex-husband was a weapons enthusiast. They would go shooting on weekends. Drive to a gravel pit. Other people shot there. Couples. Families.

—Come for a drink, George says.
　—Well—
　—Don't beg off.
The bar. Clean. Sunlight on the polished wood, brass and porcelain tap handles.
　—Dry martini, no olive.
Beer. Tap is cheaper. George will pick it up. Imports.

He went to weapon collectors' shows. Hobby. But what he brought home. Swords. Maces. A suit of armor, the whole thing. He had always liked fantasy books. Began to talk about torture.

Neat bottle with harp. 355 milliliters.
　—Let's not waste time, George says.
　—What's your story?
　—What's your gripe?
　—Why blame me?

He would not answer the door. Left guns and ammunition all over the place. Quit working. Would not go out.
　When she left, he shook his head and said, you too?
　She would call. He would never answer.

—Lone wolf, starvation, George says. Save it for the movie. Anyway, I'm bought out. Company got me, corporation got them. Remember the pictures of the food chain in your sixth grade science book? The fish?

.   .   .

The printer's sign is mounted on a steel reinforcing rod:

PRINTING

WEDDING INVITATIONS

BUSINESS FORMS

CARDS

NOTARY PUBLIC

STAMPS MADE

A tall man. Bald. Stooped among the yellowed sam-ples. Requesting the pleasure of your presence. Manager of sales. Small black press a dinosaur of science and indus-try. The printer's eyes like dull marbles in the skull.

—It won't be long, he says.

She got worried about him. It seemed normal that he would not answer the phone until she realized how abnor-mal that was. She wanted to be sure he was all right. He could have been dead. Suicide. Or hurt himself while he was drunk and bled to death in the bathroom.

Her brother went along to warn her if there was some-thing she should not see.

Her ex was sitting on the floor with a circle of guns around him: rifles, pistols, shotguns. Pint of whiskey in one hand. Empty tallboys scattered about.

He went for a revolver. Slipped out of his hand, fell on the shag carpet. Grabbed it. Slipped again. Hand on the walnut grips. He mumbled.

She was afraid it would go off.

Told him it was her. Told him everything was okay.

.   .   .

—The last I heard he was in California in a cooperative living situation.

    —A commune?

    —They don't use that word.

    —One big house?

    —They have four or five townhouses.

Eddie pushes a cart through the halls, filling it with trash bags. He goes to the basement.

    The incinerator man mumbles.

    Eddie takes an empty cart.

    —Burn the syringes, the incinerator man says.

The printer's teeth a twisted muddle.

    —Custom stamp.

    —How much?

    —Seventeen even. What do you do?

    —I'm an artist.

    —You don't see that much nowadays.

—Have another, George says. Maybe a snack? By the way, describe every feeling you've ever experienced: emotional, psychological, physical.

The stamp makes a neat black Uzi.

—He makes things, George says. I sell things.

    —Past and future.

    —Simple.

—Practice evasion, George says.

                ·   ·   ·

Bordered by the crossed black Uzis, the architecture of landscaping, trimmed hedges and shaped trees, flower beds outlined in plastic pipe. The flagstones of the walk are sharp, but muted in tone. They lead to the cedar walls and paneled doors of the townhouses. Perspective is perfect, the clarity almost superreal. An orange tree dominates the foreground, its ripe fruit shining in the sun.

—Be someone else, George says.

III

The Concealment Artist walks onto the stage. The auditorium is dark, the audience silent. It is hard to tell, from the seats below the stage, the size of the man. Well-proportioned, yes, but tall or short is impossible to say. His clothing is undistinguished: jeans, sweatshirt, corduroy sports coat, desert boots. His hair is brown. He is clean-shaven.

—All names are aliases, he says, to sparse laughter, the odd clap and whistle.

—Where's the screen? Eddie says.

—What? says Dolores.

—Isn't there a video?

—I don't know. My sister won the tickets. I thought you'd like it.

The stage is barren except for a velvet-covered stand. A woman, blonde, muscled, attractive in a huge and theatrical way in her spangled magician's assistant's suit, brings the weapons to the table. They shine—the steel mini-derringer, the chrome twenty-five auto, the ten-shot twenty-two semi, the stainless thirty-eight special, the chopped forty-five, the full-sized wonder nine—all laid out like toys beneath a Christmas tree. She goes behind the curtains, reappears with a wooden easel, and places a poster on it. A musical flourish from the 1890's plays. The poster says CONCEALMENT ARTIST. Scattered applause. The man on stage bows. Raises his hands. The sleeves of his jacket fall away from his forearms, exposing vague tattoos.

—My background is best left to the imagination, the artist says. As are all of ours.

He twists, turns, spirals. The guns disappear. Enter two men in police uniforms. The artist places his hands palms down on the stand, bends forward.

One policeman draws his revolver and holds it on the artist. The other policeman frisks the artist, comes up empty-handed. The policemen switch roles. The second cop finds nothing. Applause. The artist bows.

The woman brings out a unicycle. The artist mounts to applause. He goes forward and backward, stands on the pedals, almost flips. No weapon falls. He leaps like a ballerina, lands tiptoed on the seat of the rolling unicycle. It is only an instant, but the effect seems longer. He hops off, bows, and flips into a series of quick cartwheels around the stage.

While he towels off with a silk scarf, the spangled lady pushes a safe on stage. She handcuffs the artist and pushes him inside. His head sticks out through a hole in the top. She cuts the safe, and apparently the artist, in half with an acetylene torch and wheels the lower half of the safe around the stage. The upper half hangs fixed in the air. The artist's eyes follow the progress of the lower half. His head and the top of the safe spin slowly, then quickly. The woman places the lower half beneath the upper half. The upper half drops slowly, still spinning, and screws itself onto the lower half. The artist's head disappears into the safe. He pops the door open and leaps out, free of the handcuffs.

The woman sets up a card table and two folding chairs and exits center stage. The Concealment Artist sits down. A screen drops from the ceiling. A picture of the President is projected on the screen. The Concealment Artist stands. The picture changes. Now it is a senator.

The artist stands in the light of the projection. He strikes the eighteen martial postures. The projector shuts down. The theater is pitch black. Eddie coughs. Someone answers with a far away cough. Silence. A long pause. The lights come up.

Eddie finds himself on stage. He scans the audience but cannot see beyond the third row. Dolores is lost to him. The lights are hotter than he imagined. The Concealment Artist looms large. He is gigantic, six-four or -five with upper arms as big as Eddie's thighs and hands like cafeteria trays. He invites Eddie to frisk him. Eddie gives him a perfunctory patting down, hands trembling.

The audience giggles. The artist says something Eddie does not catch. The giggles become a roar of laughter. The artist pushes Eddie to a folding chair. Eddie sits at the card table. The artist walks center stage. The lights go down; a spot hits the artist. Eddie looks at the vinyl table top. It is torn and has been patched with a piece of duct tape. He looks up—dark, empty space. The artist produces the pistols, beginning with the forty-five and working his way down to the humble mini-derringer. Each comes out of his clothes easily, naturally, with a little flourish of his hand. Burst of applause.

Eddie cannot help but be a little amazed. True, his frisk was not much, but he clearly passed his hands over some of the guns without feeling them. The woman looks as though she has been gilded—a walking statue—until Eddie realizes she is wearing a gold body stocking beneath her spangled suit. She pushes a cart with several assault rifles on it.

The Concealment Artist asks Eddie to blindfold him. Eddie gets up and ties a heavy black cloth around the man's head. The artist says something about the weapons being specially licensed. The audience titters. The woman pushes a plastic stopwatch on stage. It is a meter in diameter and has the name of a Japanese manufacturer imprinted on its base. She calls go and starts the clock.

The artist's hands dazzle as they disassemble and reassemble the rifles. In thirty seconds he is finished with one; by the time two minutes are up, he has done all five. He strips off the blindfold and bows. The blindfold unfurls to become a cape. He drapes the cape over his arm and thrusts a rifle into it.

The artist waves the cape; the rifle is gone. He quickly dispatches the other rifles as the crowd cheers. The house lights come up. The Concealment Artist bows and leaves the stage. Applause.

Eddie sits at the card table. The audience gives the artist a standing ovation. People chant MORE, MORE, MORE. The artist trots onstage, the cape around his neck.

He gestures broadly at Eddie. —I have forgotten my poor volunteer. He walks to the card table. —I'll make it up to you. What is your name?

—Eddie Niijls.

—Interesting. Russian? Perhaps Finnish?

—I'm not sure. Irish, I heard, from when the Danes were there. Maybe it's not true.

—They deigned name you? The artist winks to the crowd. —Eddie, you've been a great help, and in return, I'll tell your fortune.

He takes Eddie's hand. —I find this method best. That is, without splitting entrails. He squints at Eddie's palm. —Hmmm. Troubling. Perhaps you have used some solvent? The lines are indistinct. Are you, by chance, under a physician's care? No? Maybe you should be.

The crowd laughs.

—Oh, the artist says, I'm sure it's quite harmless. Suppose we try a more oracular approach. What to use? My sticks are at home, and I never carry coins during a performance.

He reaches into Eddie's shirt. —Ah, what's this?

He pulls out a handful of cartridges. Eddie stares at them. They are as big as his fingers, long brass cases with copper-jacketed bullets ending in sharp tips of exposed lead. The artist swings the cartridges overhead, lets them go. They fall in a pattern on the card table.

—Khan, the artist says.

Eddie opens his mouth.

The artist puts up his hand. —A cave within a cave.

The lights go down.

—Evil despite sincerity.

Eddie looks at his shoes.

—Some deliverance. No error. Filling with water, but this line shows you have yet to go under. Some hope. Twice or thrice bound in the thickets of thorns. You find no way. There will be great evil.

Applause. Lights up. The artist exits. Eddie sits at the table, his head in his hands, as people leave.

IV

Eddie takes the bus home. He sees the flashing lights of fire trucks and police cars.

The barrier an official line of yellow plastic. Security men in uniforms.

—Can I get in?

—Why?

—I live here.

—Which is yours?

—One-O-three.

—You're lucky. It was across the hall. How well do you know your neighbor?

—Not at all.

—You don't know anything, right? You never notice people coming and going, or what the neighbor does, or what model car he drives, or his license number, right?

—Sorry.

—Look, man, this is a community. Join up.

—When can I get in?

—There's an investigation in progress. You don't have any oily rags, do you? Leave your name and address.

—But where will I stay?

—Your problem. Don't make us come looking for you.

The man at the desk is friendly. His rich accent puts Eddie at ease. There is free cable.

It is colder. Winter coming on early maybe. Cold snap, Eddie thinks. He will say that next time he talks to somebody. "Cold snap, huh?" This is what he'll say. Or, "Front moved down from Canada."

The line at the building gets longer and longer. The building's windows are covered, and the burnt-out doorway is sealed with steel mesh. The heavily armed guards have a hut-like sentry box. They talk to people through a sliding window.

He thinks of the motel manager as Mr. Haji. Once a week, Mr. Haji asks about money. Eddie looks at the floor and says he has been promised a voucher.

The food does not come by voucher. An old woman shows Eddie where to get it. He meets her in line.

They give him a set amount. Mostly in cans. Cereals are his favorite. Oatmeal and white flour and corn meal. He works every day. With limited success, it is true. Bad materials are at fault: he glues the cereals to a piece of cardboard with toothpaste to simulate the cool tones of a suburban townhouse.

One day they give him a coat. A big stormcoat with frayed cuffs and lambswool lining and wide lapels. Old, but serviceable and warm.

Eddie has a plan. When the voucher comes through and he is able to pay Mr. Haji, he will need his own place. A base of operations.

He dreams now vividly. Of a woman. Dolores. And not Dolores. The dreams are passionate, varied, erotic.

Mr. Haji lends him a lint brush. The sky is threatening. Eddie carefully brushes the stormcoat inside and out. Tomorrow might be warm. He wishes he had a necktie.

The pants and shirt they gave him are okay, but a tie would be nice.

He will get land. Not much. Anywhere. An acre of woods or part of a field. Dig a well. Outhouse, no plumbing. Do without electricity. Maybe go south, save on heat. He could build it. From plywood. From tarpaper.

The first snowfall. Large, delicate flakes melt in Eddie's hair. He walks past the silent machine shops and warehouses and factories. Eddie enters a neighborhood of small houses with dirty, warped façades. Junkers line the streets and block driveways. Chained dogs bark.

He crosses the division street, a broad avenue. Eddie remembers his building. The one before. The artists' co-op. That building is far. Eddie grows tired.

Sometimes he forgets what he must do. He must get money from George.

An area of shops. Neat storefronts with colorful displays. Eddie looks for patterns. Navaho designs are big. He straightens the lapels of his stormcoat. He would like a hat, felt, with an inch-and-a-half brim, but he does not see any. They could be out. Some neckties with Van Goghs and Gauguins on them. Imports from Guatemala.

Eddie looks for George's Mercedes. Some of the stores look a little shabby. Cracked bricks; some mortar worn away. A gutted shop. Others burnt out. Smashed windows. Posters advising citizens to turn in arsonists.

George's gallery is empty. Bands of masking tape form X's on the windows. A sign gives a new address.

He could get there, maybe, by bus. Two transfers or

three. It is a development. An old brewery. Shops and restaurants. Café tables with Cinzano umbrellas in the center court. He could sit at a table. First stop by the tobacco shop for Balkan Sobranies, then a pint of Irish lager and a snack, say calamari. Someone might stop. Friends of George, people he used to know. Maybe Dolores. She would not. Odds a million to one against. Have a look at the stores. Buy a new suit. Call her. Tell her to come by. Have a drink. She could laugh and be happy.

—You lost? Uniform. Riot stick.

—No.

—I think so. You wouldn't stand here otherwise.

—Thank you, I'm going. Thank you.

He is not sure when school gets out, but it is wise to detour around a few neighborhoods. The snow is heavier.

Eddie's feet are numb; the brogans they gave him soaked through. He is not sure where he is. He sees the printer's house. Eddie stumbles up the steps and tries to open the storm door, but his hands cannot work the handle. He keeps trying. His hands flop on the door like dying fish.

—My old customer. How can I help?

Eddie shakes. A press clacks as it prints out invitations. The printer pushes Eddie into a chair and brings him coffee.

—As you see, I'm working today. Money coming in.

The house does not have to be much. The snow has slowed. He has a map the printer made for him. Eddie finds his way to his old neighborhood. If he can get land,

the slab will be easy. It is getting dark as he nears his
building. Framing he can do, and maybe use prefab joists.
The ground vibrates. Sounds like metal tearing. Get a
small wood stove, the basic model. There is a string of
lights above the street. Some spotlights up ahead. The
walls could be canvas. Old paintings. Staple them to both
sides of the studs and stuff rags between them for insula-
tion. Bulldozers push mounds of debris. Eddie's building
is gone.

V

Eddie cannot go out. Sometimes someone comes to his
door and knocks gently. Eddie stays in bed with the pillow
over his face.

—Mr. Niijls, are you all right?

Eddie is tired and confused. He opens the door.

—You are ill? Mr. Haji says.

—No, no. I'm fine.

—I have disturbed you?

—No. No. Fine.

—Have you eaten?

—Yes. Fine. Fine. Eddie points to an empty soup can.

—I have bad news. You must leave tomorrow.

—The voucher—

—I am sorry.

Eddie goes to the bus stop. Most of his work was destroyed. But George must have some of it. Eddie has his
work-in-progress in the suitcase Mr. Haji gave him. That
could give him an entry—credibility.

·   ·   ·

The building is not as he envisioned it. The shops sell women's clothing or overpriced novelties. The restaurants sell French-inspired fast food. There is a lot of wrought iron and plastic ivy.

A drink, perhaps, to bolster him.

There are not any bars.

The art at George's strikes him strange. Wildlife and Indians and textured neutral hangings. People on horses. Horses on plains.

—What is it? George says. He wears a dark suit with a wide chalk stripe. British-looking.

—You remember me?

—No. Eddie? The stone rolled away and Eddie returned? Extraordinary. Come.

He leads Eddie to an office. Blond desk, couch and matching chairs, patterned carpet.

—Everyone thought you were gone. There was some talk of California, I believe.

—I lost my place.

—Really? George sits down on the desk.

—Then I had to leave.

George nods. —Well, what is it? The help? Cash? Will that settle us up? A job? Sorry, we're fully staffed. Take some of your work? Look at me, Eddie.

—I'm working on this thing, Eddie says. It's rough.

George sucks in his cheeks.

—I went to see the Concealment Artist.

—Shit, George says. What's an auto in the sock?

Eddie looks at the watch hanging from George's vest.

—Concentrate, Eddie.

.   .   .

George does not look like George. Same suit, but the man is radiant. Gentle. Warm.

EDDIE: Who're you?

B.O.S.: A businessman. Perhaps a bit more. You might say I'm something of a symbol to many people.

EDDIE: The Businessman of the Saved.

B.O.S.: Yes.

EDDIE: And you have a message?

B.O.S.: You came to me.

EDDIE: The message that will transform the world.

B.O.S. *(Laughing)*: We must take the world as we find it.

EDDIE: Yes.

B.O.S.: This is not to say we desire stagnation.

EDDIE: The world as it is, only transformed.

B.O.S.: You're close, but while change is the only constant in the global marketplace, complete transformation is an abstraction. We're looking at reorganization in some localities and an inherent stagnation in others. Patterns of commercial transfer. Labor as a commodity. A movable base that allows for flexibility as resource and labor components are exhausted.

EDDIE: Exhausted?

B.O.S.: Have to run. Put together a package. Come along. Listen. Learn.

The Businessman of the Saved leads Eddie through corridors lined with offices and abstract paintings. They attend meetings. At length they reach the limousine. A chauffeur in a natty black uniform holds the door.

The car is like the loss of a half-remembered love as one wakes from dreaming.

EDDIE: Foreign job?

B.O.S.: Multinational. Body, engine, drivetrain—Japanese. American interior. Check the dash.

Eddie looks. Rich light shines through concentric crystalline spheres. The spheres rotate, emitting eerie, beautiful music. Small lights flicker. Devices as complex and delicate as gyroscopes spin to the music's rhythm.

EDDIE: Amazing. Where?

B.O.S.: Switzerland. Watch business isn't what it used to be, but the market sees no talent is wasted.

The condo is at the top of the tallest building in the world. They ride up in a glass express elevator. The chauffeur, Fritz, stands at attention near the control panel.

One wall of the condo is glass: it overlooks the downtown. The carpet is white, the furniture contemporary. Fritz comes out in a butler's uniform with a tray of cocktails.

The Businessman of the Saved motions Eddie to a chair. Fritz brings cigars. Eddie selects one. Fritz lights it with a silver lighter. The Businessman of the Saved picks up the remote control for the wide-screen high-definition TV.

B.O.S.: All this could be yours.

Eddie reclines, sinks into the warm leather. The Businessman of the Saved flips on the TV. Football. Eddie finishes his drink. Fritz removes the empty glass. The Businessman of the Saved nods. Fritz brings dry beer in crystal steins.

B.O.S.: There's the game, eh?

Eddie's mouth is full of dry beer. He nods.

B.O.S.: Spin the wheel.

He hits the remote. A video comes on. The dancing woman has long, tightly curled hair.

B.O.S.: Behind the curtain.

Eddie is entranced by the dancer.

B.O.S.: Look, you deserve better.

Other videos. Fritz brings more beer and some snacks: chicken wings, herring, crudités, sushi, pickled okra, caviar, shrimp, escargots, oysters.

B.O.S.: Lost or stolen.

The game comes on again.

B.O.S.: Security. Look to the future.

Eddie's cigar has gone out. He turns his head to the side and closes his eyes.

B.O.S.: Over fifty years' experience.

Eddie hears music, but he cannot open his eyes.

B.O.S.: Clink of fine crystal.

Someone running for a touchdown, the announcer's voice rising, the roar of the crowd.

B.O.S.: The envy of the world.

Eddie wakes. Fritz is carrying him toward a microvan. He has been wrapped in a blanket.

—What happened?

—You had a little spell.

The van drops Eddie downtown.

VI

Eddie suffers misfortune. Three men with a butcher knife rob him. He has two dollars. He gives them the money and his digital watch and tells them that is it. They take his shoes. There is snow on the ground. Eddie steals clothes from a laundromat dryer and wraps his feet. He begs enough for a small hamburger and coffee and keeps on, following the freeway towards the printer's house.

Eddie avoids people.

.   .   .

The printer is on the porch. Two bulbs burn in the ceiling fixture. Eddie pounds on the door.

—Are you all right? The printer looks at Eddie's feet.

—Yeah. The rags are soaked with blood. Eddie looks out at the pink footprints, the history of his progress, in the snow. —I'll be fine.

—Uh huh. What is it this time?

The floor is covered with parts—metal type, heavy levers, intricate gears and toothed flywheels, frames. Dead-looking steel or cast iron.

—I see you're busy.

The printer bends over a table, adjusts a goose-necked lamp, picks up an Allen wrench. He squints, frowns, steps back. The wrench hangs loosely in his hand.

—Maybe you could spare me a minute? Eddie says.

The printer crosses the room, takes a monocle from the desk, claps it on his eye. —You're back. Tell me something that wasn't inevitable. He smiles weakly, his large eyes watery and gentle. —Have some coffee. He motions toward the percolator.

—MISTER COME BACK NOW, the printer says. MISTER I ONLY VISIT WHEN I'M IN TROUBLE BECAUSE I DON'T WANT MY FANCY FRIENDS TO SEE.

The printer's hand sweeps over the destroyed presses. —All in pieces and you're all of a piece. And you like a son to me.

EDDIE: The Businessman of the Damned.

B.O.D.: Your useless education was purchased with toil and sweat. Never forget that.

EDDIE: Have I?

B.O.D.: Have I told you never to forget that?

EDDIE: The press?

B.O.D.: Not beyond repair. New models cost a fortune.

EDDIE: All those pieces.

B.O.D.: Got to fix her. That baby's got to last another season at least.

EDDIE: Scrimp . . . long-range . . . capital investment.

B.O.D.: Don't spout theory; we've work to do. Look at this place. Nobody gave me a handout, mister, nor a leg up, nor a bloody fucking bootstrap to pull. Uh, no offense.

EDDIE: Huh?

B.O.D.: I'd always dreamed you would return, and the old woman dreamed so as well, God rest her soul. Gave us comfort on many a cold night.

EDDIE: What?

B.O.D. (A tear rolls down his cheek): It's true all this doesn't look like much compared to life in the army, I mean in the city, I mean in those beer commercials.

EDDIE: It's cold in here.

B.O.D. (Tenderly): And a cold coming you had of it. Take some of those lousy rags from your feet and stuff 'em in the window there. That'll cut the wind at least.

Eddie does as he is told.

B.O.D.: Still and all, we'll get her into shape. When she's a going concern, you'll feel like a new man. (He takes up a rasp) Many of the parts are usable yet, and those that aren't we'll machine ourselves.

EDDIE: I don't know.

B.O.D.: Don't expect you to. You're only an apprentice.

EDDIE: A printer's devil?

B.O.D.: You'll be expected to demonstrate your loyalty to the firm. No wages. But maybe we can find you some socks, eh? *(B.O.D. laughs heartily)* No, just joshing you. You'll have your socks, and boots as well. You'll have your keep.

EDDIE: Um.

B.O.D.: You're home.

Eddie's feet heal in the boots. There is never enough light for the work. The food is monotonous: oatmeal, black bread, beans, rice. The stray chunk of stringy meat. Weak coffee. Tap water. They work twelve hours a day. There is no clock in the shop. Eddie sleeps on a mat in the corner, his stormcoat for a blanket.

He studies the Businessman of the Damned's visage. The sickly pallor. Thin hair. Rotten teeth. Bloodshot eyes. There are no mirrors in the shop.

The door bursts open. Fritz in an iridescent black uniform, a long stiletto in hand. He glances around, raises the shades, closes the knife and puts it in his jacket. The Businessman of the Saved enters.

B.O.D.: A great honor.

B.O.S.: Greetings. *(He sees Eddie)* How could you cross alive into this gloom?

EDDIE: Hello.

B.O.D.: Don't mind him, he's learning the trade.

B.O.S.: Ah, the trade.

B.O.D.: To carry on when I'm gone.

B.O.S.: Just so. Fritz!

Fritz opens a briefcase and shows its contents to the Businessman of the Damned. Eddie moves over to the type cabinet. Fritz and the Businessman of the Damned converse. The Businessman of the Saved sidles up to Eddie.

B.O.S.: Part of the family tradition?

EDDIE: Well . . .

B.O.S.: I should have brought milk. Meat. Blood. What have you been feeding on?

EDDIE: Oh.

B.O.S.: Destined to grinding labors like my own in the sunny world?

EDDIE: I had to go somewhere.

B.O.S.: Not so bad a hole as many one could fall into. But what future?

EDDIE: It's temporary.

B.O.S.: Without saying. Communications, what better? But these relics? In the satellite era?

EDDIE: What else is there?

FRITZ: All finished here, sir.

B.O.S.: Good.

The Businessman of the Saved claps the Businessman of the Damned on the back, shakes his hand, slips him a fifty-dollar bill.

FRITZ *(To Eddie)*: Better . . . sod . . . iron rations . . . Lord, it . . . exhausted dead.

B.O.S. *(To Eddie in stage whisper)*: You're surprised? The old bastard's the father of us all.

B.O.D.: Thank you. This is a day we'll long remember. A visit by a personage of Your Eminence's stature. And the work. We're not down to our last crust, but close enough, sir, close enough. Good for the lad as well, to see the caliber of people a businessman encounters. Puts me in mind of the boy's dear mother . . .

EDDIE *(A tear rolls down his cheek)*: My mother . . .

B.O.D.: I'm not alone, sir, in feeling it would be an appropriate memorial to yourself and your outstanding service to the community.

B.O.S.: There was some talk of an equestrian statue. But it's not about recognition.

B.O.D.: Indeed.

B.O.S.: It's about love.

B.O.D.: Hark you, lad. Work and love.

B.O.S.: Love and work.

FRITZ *(A tear rolls down his cheek)*: It is not possible to live without love.

Fritz and the Businessman of the Saved go out the door and down the steps.

EDDIE: . . . yes I will. Yes.

VII

The truth falls on Eddie like the weight of the world. He must cross the city and go to Dolores. There is no room for weakness.

As the printer sleeps, Eddie rises from his mat. He thinks about leaving a note, but no language will soften the blow for the old man.

He takes a crowbar, compensation for his labors, and slips out. A knife would be better, but the old man keeps the obvious weapons locked up. The crowbar serves. It is eighteen inches long and has a comfortable heft.

He will move at night, save the days for rest. Eddie will do what he has to do. Everything else is secondary. He checks parked cars for valuables.

A man carrying a heavy grocery bag. No one else on the street. Eddie moves towards the entryway of an apartment building.

—Yo. Hold up, the man says.

—What? Eddie says. Hand on the crowbar inside his coat.

—Hold up. The man limps toward him. —I'm hurt.

—Come closer, you'll be dead. Eddie brings out the crowbar. —I'll fuck you up.

—Help me. The man holds up the bag. —I'll share.

—Give me the bag, Eddie says.

—Help me or leave me; I keep the bag.

—I could kill you and take it.

The man looks at the ground.

Everything comes out of the bag: antiseptic, ointment, gauze, bandages. The wound is in the thigh, an ugly puncture, but whether it is a gun or a knife job, Eddie cannot say.

The man will not tell. —Just help. You'll get your just reward.

—What if there's a projectile in the tissue?

—My problem.

—I'm no doctor—

—Then shut up.

Eddie cleans the wound, packs it, wraps it securely. He is careful not to cut off the circulation. —You'll be okay if there's no infection.

The man opens the sack. —What do you want?

—Got a car in there?

Bagman laughs. —Here. He hands Eddie a half-pint of whiskey.

—That's it?

—All right. He gives Eddie a joint.

—And?

—Here. He gives Eddie a russet potato.

Eddie lights the joint and opens the bottle. They smoke and drink in the doorway.

Bagman explains everything: Eddie's problem is that he does not have any money. Maybe Bagman will take Eddie in. Eddie is grateful and wary. They sleep bundled in rags in a refrigerator box beneath a railway trestle. Bagman keeps a small chrome-plated revolver to discourage the inhabitants of the neighboring hovels from coming by. Eddie has not forgotten Dolores.

Bagman's leg is almost healed. He tells Eddie to wait by the box while he goes spotting. Eddie waits all day. He bakes potatoes in the embers of a garbage fire.

Bagman returns at dusk. They eat.

—Let's go.

—Where?

—Watch. I'll show you what to do.

They walk for miles through blocks of concrete flats. It is dark when Bagman stops. He hops into a window well and pries the security bars from the window frame with a flat piece of steel. He makes a large X on the glass with masking tape, delivers a sharp rap with the steel. The glass breaks neatly. Most of it pulls out on the tape.

Eddie follows him through the window. Bagman holds the steel like a bludgeon, checks the rooms. A night light is on in the bathroom. Bagman ransacks the bureau. Eddie hesitates. Bagman points at the closet. Eddie sorts through the hanging clothes, the shoes on the floor. He does not see anything of value, just clothes, shoes.

Bagman fills his pockets and leads Eddie into the front room. They are disconnecting the speaker wires. The door is kicked in. Uniformed men. Shotgun pointed at Eddie. He grabs Bagman. Pulls. The gun goes off. Bagman in front of Eddie. Sagging.

Eddie unharmed. —Small shot, he says.

Bagman falls.

Eddie is in the window frame.

Out.

Running.

Eddie waits in the box. He is afraid he is covered with blood. There are tests which could link him to Bagman's death. He strips off his clothes. The smallest trace of organic material, a drop of blood, bit of tissue, a hair, is enough to hang him. Eddie cannot find a trace.

He remembers something about bloody footprints. Tracks. He checks his boots. No blood.

He waits and hopes.

Sirens and shouts wake him. The noise is meaningless. Then he knows they are after him. Bagman, if alive, ratted him. Eddie wriggles out of the box. Shots and screams. He runs with the neighbors from nearby boxes and hootches. They move toward the bottom of the gorge, hoping to get across and get lost on the opposite slope. The uniformed men follow in a line. Their pace is leisurely. They set shacks on fire, reload their automatic pistols and jam birdshot into their shotguns, joke. Everything is easy. A bugle sounds far off. Olive-drab helicopter twirls overhead. Eddie dives for the opposite slope.

The houses are large stone or brick or mock-Tudor structures with high walls around them. The streets are empty

—Hey. A child's voice.

—Hey, Dad.

Eddie opens his mouth. His jaw cracks. Sharp pain in the joint. Flapping tongue, numb lips. He gives off a harsh rasp.

The snap of an automatic pistol's slide. —I'll take care of this, Son.

—Don't, Eddie says. I'll go. When I catch my breath. He tries to sit up. —I'm hurt.

—You're on my property. Move or I'll kill you.

—Please. Let me stay. Until I heal. I'll watch the place.

—Impractical.

—Can we cut off his eyelids, Dad?

—Not now, Son.

—Please, Eddie says.

—Go get the manacles out of my toolbox.

Eddie's left wrist is chained to an iron ring in the wall. He sleeps. When he is not sleeping, he watches. There is milky light with shapes in it. He grows thin but keeps sinking through the snow and rotting leaves to the earth. Eddie feels himself unfleshed. His skeleton leaves a hard silver imprint on the ground, a permanent image that freezes and thaws will never eradicate. He knows where the knife is in him. The point is stuck in one of his ribs. Perhaps the blade will dissolve by spring and he will be free. No one disturbs his peace.

VIII

Rain falls gently, then in long lines. Sheets. He does not sink. A wet dog howls. The rains slack off. A sunny day. A couple more. Grass and weeds come up. The mud dries. He sits. One day he stands. Walks. Until the chain stops him. He goes back to the wall. Out again. And back.

They lengthen the chain. Later take it off. Give him some cord and a plastic tarp. He rigs the tarp, attaching it to the wall and garage. He does not enter the house; it never occurs to him. The boy brings him things: cold coffee, a cigarette, bit of chocolate, half can of imported beer.

Sometimes in the cool of the evening, he walks with the man. Other times, he squats beneath his hootch and scratches strange glyphs in the dirt with a stick. The boy watches. He shows the boy things—perspective, vanishing point. The boy brings a pencil stub and paper.

The man mentions the sketches. He found the boy in the boy's room, drawing. The man examined the pictures closely; any good parent would do the same. Frankly, the man was impressed with the quality of the work.

Perhaps some arrangement can be made. Say the man were to supply the artist materials, working space, and his keep. In the house. The artist could be a sort of temporary member of the family.

Of course, there are limits. The artist is a craftsman, no doubt, but this is not a commission to run riot. The family is primary, and everyone must know his place in it.

The artist is deloused, shaved, barbered. The man gives him an old suit. The artist finds a five-dollar bill in the vest pocket. The man leads the artist downstairs to a subbasement. Square room with crumbling limestone walls. Bare bulb. Metal cot, no mattress, wire net instead of springs. Wooden table. Scrap lumber stacked in the corner.

.   .   .

Studies are made. Standard practice. Cartoons. Not in the pejorative sense. Materials are in short supply. And time is valuable. Not that he is to rush. What is wanted is a quality product. Something to hang on to. Something that will increase in value. But it has to be in one take. For now, he will have snapshots to work from. Retrain his eye.

They pose in the living room. The man and boy stand. The woman sits between them in a Victorian easy chair.

The artist wants the boy in the foreground.

—We've made our decision, the man says.

—But—

—I believe we have a verbal contract. When you were hungry, as it were, you voiced no objections.

—It's just a suggestion.

—Very well. The man turns to his family. —There's a suggestion.

—Uh.

—Please proceed.

—The boy could go here. It would make balance.

—Balance is not the point.

—In a way it is.

—He'll obscure his mother. What sort of family history will this be with the boy's mother only half there?

—There's a precedent.

—Really?

—Traditional. The boy projecting into the future.

—Never heard of such a thing.

—You've seen it. The holy family.

—Holy family?

—Imagine.

—Yes, yes.

.   .   .

He gets their shapes. The man brings lights and paint to the artist's room. A photo of the family is blown up to poster size in case there is a problem. Brushes are supplied as needed, but the artist has only one canvas.

The artist roughs in the rows of flowers on the wallpaper. He puts in the chandelier and pedestal table, the bust of Caesar and the aquarium. He is doing the ceiling, spreading some flat white with a putty knife, when he tears the canvas.

The man is not happy. There are three tears now, above the family and on either side of them. The artist assures the man this happens all the time. What is needed is a bit of canvas so he can patch the tears. None of this will be visible to the untrained eye.

He plasters Chinese white over the torn areas and puts his work on the patches: birds and reptiles, the sun and moon in various relations, a dog howling at a ladder that reaches into the night sky. Before the paint has completely dried, he patches over the images with fresh canvas.

A man's face, a heart, a playing card. He blanks them out. Tigers, foreign gods, guns, gangsters of earlier eras, house plans, diamond-shaped convergences of lines with spheres at each intersection, precious stones. Dolores.

The artist awakes.
—If you're so goddamn fucking intelligent, the man says, so bloody fucking superior, why do you live in my storeroom?

The boy hops up and down. The woman weeps, her face covered.

The man turns towards the boy, inadvertently pointing the pistol at him. —For the love of God, settle down.

He points the pistol at the artist.

—Get out.

The artist pulls on his trousers.

The man racks the slide. —Now.

The artist puts his feet in his shoes and grabs his clothes. He glances at the painting.

—Move your ass.

The artist realizes he has no shirt. He puts on his vest and jacket and jams his tie in his pocket. He buys a pack of cigarettes and a beer at a minimart. Two pay phones are mounted on the outer wall of the store. He steps to the nearest phone. The receiver is missing, the silver cord cut.

IX

The sergeant buzzes Eddie in. He limps, feet blistered, half-starved, over the threshold.

—Number? the sergeant says.

Eddie blinks.

—Give me the number, the sergeant says. The one you called.

Eddie stammers out the number.

The sergeant shakes his head. —Pathetic.

Another room: paper-covered examining table, scale, desk, sink, shiny wastebasket. A man in a labcoat comes in. —You're a relative?

—Uh, Eddie says.

—Here for a checkup? Company physical?

—They said wait. He gives the man a form.

—You? The man takes Eddie's pulse. Feels his biceps. —You must have some kind of big-time connection to get you across.

—Well—

—Don't tell me; somebody made a call. He thumps Eddie's chest, listens to Eddie's heart. —It's pumping. I can certify that.

—That's—

—That's enough, huh? He hits Eddie's knee with a hammer. —Mostly we don't bother with this anymore. He pulls back Eddie's eyelid. —In your case, I think a conservative approach appropriate. The man sits down at the desk. —I'm going to ask you a few questions.

They wrap cuffs around his arms and ankles, belt him to a chair, put a metal cap on his shaved head, place suction-cuplike monitors over his nipples, eyelids, kidneys, gall bladder, liver, testicles.

The leader is an older man. He tells the younger ones to shut up, goes to a wall-mounted panel, pushes some buttons. Eddie's chair slides into a rounded plastic tunnel. The tunnel fills with blue light.

The leader speaks. —Note the clarity of the image, and this without injection.

The light is constant. Eddie hears buzzing. He wishes it would stop.

—Unnecessary in a healthy individual. Notice the lesion in the lower quadrant. Hideous, yes, but we have an obligation.

The chair vibrates. Shakes. In tune with the buzz. He is shaking.

—Atoms.

—And the bone mass, disturbing. This degree of deterioration is extraordinary.

Eddie's teeth chatter.

—See to that.

The light goes white and the buzzing stops. One of the younger ones jams a piece of plastic between Eddie's teeth.

—Clear.

The hum and blue light return.

—Besides, it would take half an hour to sew the son of a bitch back on. Necrosis and near-total occlusion. Let's in for a closer look.

The light turns violet. Eddie sweats.

—Laser treatment.

—Prolonged therapy options?

—Complications?

The soles of his feet are burning. He tries to scream, but the mouthpiece gags him.

—Particles of light, yes.

Smell of burning flesh.

—Bloody shame we haven't a dissection clearance. Wind it down.

Eddie hangs limp in the restraints. He cannot get the air into his lungs.

A fast open hand to the face startles him. Eddie opens his eyes, jerks back in his chair.

The leader tosses a form onto his lap. —Don't bother to thank me.

·   ·   ·

They give him an orange jumpsuit and canvas slippers. He is blindfolded and forced onto a bench. The room moves. He realizes he is in a truck.

—Hit it running, the sergeant says.

Eddie runs. The man beside him slows down. A sergeant catches the man hard across the kidneys with a rubber truncheon.

They run everywhere. Eddie never asks questions. They clean the barracks, the yards, the roadways, the mess. Run, clean, exercise. There is a big arched sign over the gate. No one knows what it says. A few of the others disappear. Then more. Eddie notices the empty bunks. He does not ask.

The sergeants refer to them as trainees. They are allowed to play basketball on Sunday mornings. The calisthenics give way to basic martial postures.

They go to a lecture hall. A man talks. He has a wooden pointer and a tripod for displays. The lectures have titles.

—In the classroom, the sergeant says, it's theory.

They stand in ranks on the drill field. Five men have been chosen. Eddie is lucky; he is still in the ranks. The sergeant arms four of the men with truncheons, etches a square in the dirt, posts an armed man at each corner. The unarmed man is placed inside the square.

—Survival, the sergeant says, a little drill. He steps out of the square.

Eddie's legs twitch. He knows not to lock his knees. It is hot. He is thirsty.

—Often seen, the sergeant says, as dichotomy. Us and

them, he and she, I and thou. Presumes all oppositions are merely bipolar.

The sergeant lights a cigarette. —Reality is a bit more complicated. This is baby play.

The exercise begins.

A sergeant pulls him from his rack. Eddie wakes in midair, hits the concrete floor, tries to get up.

—Stay there.

Eddie hears the boots on the floor and knows they are forming a circle.

—Struggle, the sergeant says.

Eddie covers his face.

They go on and on. The sergeant screams. The others kick, shout accusations. The sergeant hits Eddie with a garbage-can lid.

Eddie remembers.

—I confess, he says.

—He confesses, the sergeant says.

The sergeant pulls Eddie up and drags him across the barracks to the concrete reeducation cell. He punches Eddie in the stomach.

—Examine your conscience, motherfucker.

No one is to blame. Eddie has accused others. He is happy to be back with the group.

He releases the safety on his weapon before the command has been given. Eddie is in the prone position. Everyone hears the click. The range sergeant kicks him in the small of the back. Eddie makes no sound.

When the others are dismissed, the sergeant calls him over to the office.

—You all right?

—I confess, Eddie says, I confess.

—Relax. It takes time. You'd be surprised how many of us started as something else.

—Really?

—Why, I was a psychologist, the sergeant says.

Although he is clumsy and slow and not the best shot, Eddie is named Most Improved Trainee and given a special honor. A dignitary is to be laid in state at Headquarters, and Eddie will serve on the honor guard. A sergeant brings him to the empty rotunda and walks him through the routine at midnight. The sound of their steps echoes through the dome.

Two medical officers wheel a casket in.

—Pop it, the sergeant says.

—Not a good idea.

—We have to be sure he's there, the sergeant says.

The doc opens the coffin. They crowd in for a look. The face has been pumped up with fluid and rouged.

—Holy shit, Eddie says. His knees lock.

—Get a hold of yourself, the sergeant says.

—Is it? Eddie says.

—We salute the uniform, not the man.

X

—There's been some talk of winding down, the group leader says. Let me tell you, we are not winding down. Economics is war by other means. We welcome this new era, this restructuring.

They huddle, lock their hands atop each others', chant

Go, go, go, push down, and break. They run past the weapons lockers, up the ramp, into the vans.

Eddie hangs on to a metal ring in the van's wall.

—Today, Jim says, a small raid.

—Small? Eddie says.

—Yeah, minimal mortality. Shouldn't be any resistance. If we take heavy fire, work your way back to the truck. Somebody'll be along for us.

A sergeant crawls back from the cab. —We're gonna hit a business. Shake 'em up.

—Who is it? somebody says.

—Some old bastard who wants to hang on. Not bad, just useless.

Eddie follows Jim out of the van. It is dark, and someone is shooting out the streetlights.

Eddie winces. —What?

—Helps the mystique, Jim says.

They move toward a house. There is a sign out front. Two men beat it with sledge hammers. The point men smash in the door with a battering ram. A figure runs from the back of the house. No one goes after him. He crosses the street and disappears into some low buildings.

They go inside the house. Broken machinery and smashed furniture. Men throw paper, dishes, clothes. Jim hands Eddie a can of spray paint.

—Do the walls.

—What do you want on them?

—Be creative.

Jim shoots a cat three times. —Always kill the pets; it's our trademark.

Eddie paints a sunburst and the words DO NOT RETURN.

He is doing EXAMINE YOUR CONSCIENCE when he hears shouts.

There is a billboard on the roof of a two-story building across the street. The printer stands on the billboard's catwalk. Eddie draws his pistol.

—Don't. Jim forces Eddie's arm down. —Light him up.

Somebody fires a flare. Eddie is entranced by the sharp trajectory of the rise, the pop of the tiny parachute, the swaying fall and carnival-like light.

—Don't be discouraged, the printer shouts.

—Idiot, Jim says.

Men carry jerrycans from the vans to the house.

—Allow for expansion, the printer says. No problems, only opportunities.

—Fire it.

—Ready on red.

—We can compete with anybody, the printer says.

—Fire in the hole.

The house explodes.

They go to restaurants and pick up envelopes, or to movies or bars or stores. The shopkeepers are accommodating; they offer Eddie and Jim gifts. Jim introduces Eddie to a tailor who alters their uniforms. Eddie starts wearing shiny, nonregulation sunglasses like Jim's.

On a pleasant evening, they work foot patrol by the river. It is dusk, and the woods on the river's banks give the air a fresh smell.

Eddie listens to the birds in the trees, lights an imported cigar. —This is why we trained so hard, eh, Jim?

—Yeah. Jim scans the area. He motions towards the

expensive houses across the road. —This is nice, but always watch the woods.

—Yeah?

—Bad people. A lot of bad people down there.

A man and a woman walk the trail beside the houses. Eddie notices their hiking shoes and colorful outfits. They are young and clean and fit. Productive people. People worth defending.

—What we ought to do, Jim says, is sweep the fuckers out once and for all.

—Yeah.

—Burn the woods. Get their fucking nest.

They walk a winding dirt road that descends to a park at the water's edge. A sign says the park closes at sundown. The gravel lot is almost empty. Rusted-out van parked near the cedar-shingled pavilion. Across the lot, a new model Japanese sedan. The hood is up and two kids lean over the engine.

—I don't like it, Jim says. Look at their shoes.

One wears scuffed boots. The other, ripped canvas sneakers. Eddie unsnaps his holster.

—Step back from the car, Jim shouts.

The kids jerk. One's arm goes back. Eddie draws his pistol. A tire iron flies, clatters short on the gravel. Jim fires. The one who threw the iron falls; the other runs. Eddie tries to get him in the sights. Jim fires. The second kid falls. Jim picks up the tire iron.

They move to the car. The battery is disconnected. The first kid is dead, chest cavity hit. The other whimpers on the ground.

—You throw things at me? Jim says.

—Let me go.

—You assault me, and I should forget it? What happened to the owner?

—Nothing.

—Then where the fuck is he?

—We never saw him.

Jim smiles at Eddie. —The owner's an invisible man. Then they attack us.

—Please, the kid says.

Jim hits him with the tire iron. —Shut up.

The kid breathes hard.

—Maybe we should give him a break, Eddie says.

—Who the fuck ever gave us a break?

They dump the bodies in the river.

Jim drives. They circle a shopping mall. Once, twice, three or four times.

—Nothing here, Eddie says.

—Yeah, Jim says. He goes up the service road to the freeway ramp. —Man, this job.

—Yeah, Eddie says.

Jim enters the freeway and zips across three lanes. Eddie looks at the speedometer. They are forty-seven over the limit.

—It's like rolling a rock up a hill, Jim says. The car moves faster, dodges a pickup, a cab, a truck full of oxygen tanks.

—Should we use the siren? Eddie says.

—You get to the top, fucker rolls back down. Know what I mean?

A light rain begins to fall. They are going a hundred and fifteen. Eddie sits straight up in his seat, feet braced against the floor.

—Like that thing at the river.

—Yeah, Eddie says.

—I know you're new, Jim says, so I don't want to say anything about it.

—Say what? Go ahead.

—I'll say this, Jim says, and we'll just leave it there. Forget it. Right?

Eddie nods.

Jim blasts by a minivan and passes a poultry truck by swerving onto the shoulder. Rocks fly.

—Don't ever go soft on me again.

Eddie realizes his mistake and works to improve. He spends time at the gym working on the killing mind.

He thinks he is alone, turns and sees Jim standing on the sidelines.

—You need me? Eddie says.

—Just stopped by. You're coming along.

—Thanks.

—Let's go for a drink.

Eddie follows Jim outside. The evening is unseasonably crisp. A few faint stars are visible.

—You know about the Lost Kings? Jim says.

—No.

Jim lights a cigarette and hands Eddie the package. —Once met an old man who'd known them. People claim they were called Kings 'cause they were the best, but that's bullshit. There were two brothers named King, and the rest got tagged that, too.

—They were aggressive. May have been five; they invented the five-man point system. They worked nights. Back then there was no real support. Maybe one helicopter for the whole city.

—One night, there was rioting. Flying columns of looters: hit here, then gone. In those warrens they had for projects. The Kings went in, kept radio contact, were mopping up. They were supposed to wait for trucks to pick 'em up in the morning. The city wasn't so built up then; there was just a field on the outskirts. They got there and called for the ride.

—The trucks go out. Half an hour between the call and the field. No Kings. They wait awhile, call more people. Not a trace. They go street to street, building to building, room to room. Bring in dynamite and wrecking balls. Field gets bigger and bigger, but they don't find anything. For a long time after that, they tested every piece of bone that washed down a gulley, but the Kings never turned up.

—Where's the field? Eddie says.

—Put it at every point on the compass. Somebody's built over it by now.

Eddie decorates the inside of his locker with pictures of women. They all look like a woman Eddie knew years ago named Dolores. When the locker is covered, he puts more pictures on the inner lid of his footlocker. Sometimes he allows himself to believe one of the women is Dolores. But only for a moment. Not always the same picture; that would be odd. It is nothing. A momentary diversion. A temporary release.

The other men have similar quirks. The men believe in luck. They carry charms: religious medals, bracelets, watches, special holsters, knives, lanyards, flashlights. Some have tattoos which are said to protect them. Jim carries a folded playing card in his wallet; no one is allowed to see its face.

Things get collected. Jim checks suspects for valuables and weapons. He keeps what he wants and throws the rest down a sewer. Jim has stuff in a rented garage across town, but that is the accumulation of years' work. The others have strongboxes or sacks in their footlockers. They bring in rings, necklaces, gold teeth, earrings.

In the beginning, Eddie is squeamish. He feels something about taking a ring from a corpse's finger. He builds a small collection.

There are riots in the Spring. Eddie is surprised by the hostility. When he and Jim take ordinary suspects, the suspects speak softly. They do not dare be noticed. The mobs are filled with hatred. Eddie knocks one down, and the guy keeps trying to fight while Eddie and some others beat him. The guy cannot hurt them; anyone with sense would roll up, cover himself. Why claw air? Sometimes Eddie and the others throw money into the crowds. Then, when they are really going good, Jim lights them up with a flamethrower.

The sector is pacified. Eddie is too tired to take off his body armor. He hits his rack and sleeps for three days.

—Hurry up, you're late, Jim says.

—What?

—There's a lecture. Jim pulls Eddie from the bunk.

—Okay. Eddie starts to unbuckle his vest.

—No time.

Jim leads Eddie through a side door. The men sit cross-legged in ranks on the polished wooden floor. The speaker is behind a bulletproof glass shield. Eddie recognizes the shining countenance. The speaker dismisses the

audience. Men filter out. The speaker walks towards
Eddie. A chauffeur follows closely behind.

—We're in for it, Jim says.

—Hello, the Businessman of the Saved says.

Eddie cannot focus his eyes. —Old problem.

Fritz bows. —Hi ya.

EDDIE: You've lost some weight?

B.O.S.: No.

EDDIE: New suit perhaps?

B.O.S.: Afraid not.

EDDIE: Tinted contacts?

B.O.S.: Naw.

EDDIE: Colored your hair?

B.O.S.: No, no, no, no.

Fritz' hand goes inside his coat.

B.O.S.: Easy. He's a friend.

EDDIE: Really?

B.O.S.: Of sorts.

Fritz salutes. Jim straightens up and salutes.

B.O.S. *(Waving them away)*: Dismissed.

Jim marches quickly out. Fritz follows.

B.O.S.: Adjusting?

EDDIE: I guess.

B.O.S.: Old Faustian bargain, what?

EDDIE: I don't know.

B.O.S.: You will.

The Businessman of the Saved walks Eddie out of the
building. Fritz waits by a sleek, severely angled helicopter.

B.O.S.: You want to go up in the bird?

EDDIE: Really?

FRITZ: The schedule?

B.O.S.: Come along; we'll up for a quick look.

They strap themselves into the plush seats. Fritz closes the hatch and takes the controls. The lift-off is smooth, forceful, like the ascent of a powerful express elevator. Eddie closes his eyes.

B.O.S.: Feeling all right?

Eddie moans.

B.O.S.: Get a grip, man.

EDDIE: Yuh.

B.O.S.: Hey, open up. Take a look out there.

Eddie looks. The city is a series of concentric rings. Smoke rises from a few ruins, but the office complexes and freeways shine in the sun, and Eddie is struck, mostly, by the beauty.

B.O.S.: Now, you see our launching pad?

EDDIE: It's different from up here.

B.O.S.: There. In the center. Prime location, no? I know what you're thinking: what about expansion? Could yesterday's prime location be dead weight today?

EDDIE: Is it possible?

The helicopter flies gracefully toward the fields and wooded hills beyond the city. Eddie looks at the new suburbs, as perfect as architects' models.

B.O.S.: Air's nicer, eh?

The rotor stops spinning.

FRITZ: Aowaowowow.

B.O.S.: Goddamnit, he has these spells.

The aircraft lists to one side.

B.O.S.: Fritz!

The helicopter loses altitude. Some houses clustered around a pond. A field beyond. The Businessman of the Saved grabs a parachute and begins strapping it on.

B.O.S.: Everything's fine. Fine, fine.

EDDIE: We're all going to die.

Eddie knows the field. He stands up. The helicopter circles, wobbles.

EDDIE: That's it.

The copter drops gently.

EDDIE: The Field of Lost Kings.

B.O.S.: Lore of the trade.

EDDIE *(He shoulders the limp Fritz aside, grabs the controls)*: We're going in.

B.O.S.: No such place. Let go.

Eddie wakes. His mouth and eyes are stuck shut. He licks his lips. Blood. —Am I dead and in hell, then?

The wreckage of the copter is a few hundred yards away in a grove of charred oak. Someone has wrapped Eddie in a parachute. He lies quietly in the silken cocoon until Jim and some others come along and load him into an ambulance. After a few days in the infirmary, he is sent back to the barracks and kept under observation.

Eddie wants to get back to work.

The cutbacks come. Men are assembled in ranks on the parade ground.

—Sorry, lads, the chief says, I held off as long as I could. It's politics, same as always, fucking politics.

Eddie is a member of the horde that snakes through a maze of tables and desks, returning issued equipment. He had not realized there were so many. He is given a cheap suit and his pay, and he manages to smuggle out a coffee can full of jewelry and other loot.

Eddie passes through the front gate. Fritz and the Businessman of the Saved stand by a refrigerated truck, handing out frozen turkeys.

B.O.S.: Not much, I know. Don't be discouraged; this is a temporary setback.

Eddie gets in line.

B.O.S.: All better, I see.

EDDIE: Listen.

B.O.S.: You were in shock. We stabilized you.

EDDIE: Fair is fair. I've served. And for my struggle?

B.O.S.: It's a crapshoot. *(He hands Eddie a turkey)* There's a good one: pop-up timer. Anyway, that's part of the price we have to pay . . .

EDDIE: I've served and I want my recompense.

B.O.S.: We saved your life, and this is gratitude?

EDDIE: Shit.

B.O.S.: You're holding up the line.

Eddie cannot help but feel he was tagged soft-hearted. Politics forced him out. He finds lodging in a boarding house and spends warm days on the stoop. When it is cold, he goes to the no-name bar down the street. He drinks beer and vodka, cheap off-brands, with the other men. As their money goes, men disappear. They do not understand their failure; the television set over the bar broadcasts strong numbers. Some of the men fight when they are drunk.

Eddie steers clear of trouble. He sells the jewelry, piece by piece, to an old woman who runs a pawnshop out of her apartment. Eddie does not linger. The woman's flesh and greasy strongbox, the smells of must and cabbage, drive him from the flat, his head filled with crazy ideas. Why not kill her and take the cash and valuables? They would be of more use to him than to the old miser.

XI

Eddie is on the sidewalk in a warehouse district. He stops to take a drink from the pint in his back pocket. A pickup with a leaning wooden topper pulls up. Eddie recognizes the old man on the passenger side.

The man rolls down the window. —Speak of the devil.

—You look worse than when I saw you last, Eddie says. What happened?

The Businessman of the Damned gets out of the truck. His suit, long out of style, is immaculate, and his ancient boots gleam. —And you're a pretty picture, eh, lad?

EDDIE: What the fuck do you know?

B.O.D.: Given up soldiering, but still a soldier's mouth. We like to think talent is all, yet temperament and environment rule as well.

EDDIE: C'mon now. *(He holds out the bottle)* Hell, have a little drink.

B.O.D.: Thanks, no. I'm on company time. By the way, I might have something for you.

EDDIE: Yeah?

B.O.D.: Stop by tomorrow.

Construction site surrounded by a cyclone fence. Eddie walks, looking for the gate. A group of men stands around a large table. Eddie starts toward the entrance. A guard steps from a box. The Businessman of the Damned, in orange bump cap, waves Eddie through.

EDDIE: Hello.

B.O.D.: Recognize it?

They stand on a lip of sand. A dirt road leads into a deep stone pit.

EDDIE: Long way down.

B.O.D.: Bulldozed the whole neighborhood.

EDDIE: How deep you say that is?

B.O.D.: Five hundred square acres, and over a thousand dwellings. Had 'em jammed in like rabbit warrens. You remember.

EDDIE: I mean straight down.

B.O.D.: Your old haunts, eh?

EDDIE: A field, then they built over it?

B.O.D.: Once maybe. What wasn't? Field, woods, glen and dale. Sweet grass in the morning when dew clings to the blades. Ah, memory. Innocent eye in the field of green. Something in that. Yes, an appeal. No, you are not the first to have these feelings. No, sir. But how could you know? If you throw out history? Have I told you, have I bored you, with the lethal consequences of forgetfulness?

EDDIE: What place is this?

B.O.D.: The plans! Get an eyeful of those blueprints; you'll see the future.

EDDIE: Plans.

B.O.D.: Would you then go backward? Unloom the looming factory wall? Spin a wheel in some cottage? What fate, that? Beyond, to sheep on some Attic hillside?

EDDIE: Forget it.

B.O.D.: All to the good.

He leads Eddie to the table, points to the plans. Lines that correspond to no scale Eddie is aware of.

B.O.D. *(Tenderly)*: You find this a bit beyond you, lad?

EDDIE: I can't.

B.O.D. *(Leading Eddie down the winding road to the pit)*: It's all right, son. Don't let it get you.

EDDIE: Maybe if I look again?

B.O.D.: It's all right. We both know the deficiencies in your education. That's no shame. If anything, I blame myself. *(Tears run down his cheeks)* The hard and lean times they were, there was not a penny to be spared.

EDDIE: Spared.

B.O.D.: I won't apologize. Don't rake me over the dead embers of yesteryear. There was always food on the table, wasn't there? Was there not? If you'd seen the rotten crusts I came to manhood upon perhaps—

Eddie stumbles, careens near the edge of the roadway, catches his balance.

B.O.D.: Quite right. Yesterday's gone and the devil take his own. I'm old.

They reach bottom: rock and sand, clumps of scrub and thistle. Eddie watches a lizard skitter under a rock. He is surprised by the heat. They walk for a long time; Eddie's sneakers fill with sand.

Men, maybe a hundred of them, move a huge slab of rock. It looks like concrete, and it is enmeshed in thick hemp cables. Foremen shout through bullhorns.

B.O.D.: Walk it, walk it.

The men pull; the slab inches forward, side-to-side.

EDDIE: Jesus Christ, it must weigh a ton.

B.O.D.: Just the thing.

EDDIE: Can't you use a machine?

B.O.D.: Sure, technology will only take you so far; it's art carries you through.

EDDIE: Oh.

B.O.D.: Imagine this a garden. Dirt, dust but momentary disruptions. But look.

The Businessman of the Damned waves his hand over the floor of the pit. The landscape is dotted with the huge concrete slabs.

B.O.D.: Each of these—now focus, boy, picture it— each of these will be a sculpture. Each sculpture sculpted by a different sculptor. A world-famous sculptor for each.

EDDIE: A sculpture garden.

B.O.D.: The beauty.

Eddie works in the quarry, shoveling gravel. A guy tells him a lot of people started in the quarry. It is always possible to move up.

The slabs stand every fifty yards or so like giant dominoes. The pit floor is level, but when the slabs are carved and the slag hauled off, the land will be graded and land-scaped. Wood-chipped paths will wind through the greenery, the gently rolling hills and flowers.

Eddie thinks as he fills wheelbarrows. His job will not last forever, and the future must hold something for him. He has credentials and talent. He will get himself apprenticed to a sculptor.

The chief's trailer is padlocked. The corrugated sheds and planning table, the guards and sentry box are gone. The gate is chained and locked. Eddie goes back to the quarry. No one is there.

He has to find the others. He runs. The sun sets. The slabs glow in the moonlight. Eddie dodges around them, stumbling. He finds himself on a plain of dirt and scrub. Beer cans and a tattered yellow rain jacket glow in the moonlight. He crashes through the brush. Brambles whip his shins, wrists, face. Up a sandy rise, down again. The faint ruts of heavy equipment. Eddie follows the trail into a chain-link fence. His face hits the metal, rebounds, hits again. Eddie crumbles.

He is thirsty. Trucks used to bring ice water in plastic coolers. Enough water for ten men in each.

He walks the fence.

Sun burns hot in this hole. Something to that. Something Eddie heard long ago about the sun or fire or X rays and some hole.

The fence gives him support.

A silver band shines. Sometimes it recedes, other times it is upon him, and Eddie gasps for air.

The water runs down his neck. Eddie shakes like a wet dog. A man up ahead leans easily over a dip in the fence. His elbow is propped on the rail, and he smokes a cigarette he holds in his free hand.

Eddie cannot believe his eyes. He has been alone in this wilderness for—for a long time. Sun started to get to him after a while. Burned.

The man wears a torn jacket that is covered with insignia and ribbons, corroded medals and rotten braid. His face is weathered and cracked, the left eye gone, the socket a mass of scar tissue with indications of crude stitching. Wound suffered years ago, no doubt. Now the mass is almost natural.

Eddie looks at the cigarette. —Have another? He raises his hands. —A bit to share? Perhaps a puff or two, or give me ends on it? If it's no trouble. Eddie walks in a small circle. —No trouble. No. No trouble. Trouble flies above us day and night. No. Eddie reverses himself, walks the circle backwards. —Flies above. Waiting.

—Ah, the man says. He shakes a cigarette half-free from the pack and holds it out to Eddie.

—God will repay you, Eddie says.

The man nods, gives Eddie a light. —Been waiting quite a while for you.

—I don't mind saying I am moved, Eddie says.

—Part of my responsibility.

—Uh?

—I walk, the man says. Security.

—Can't make you out, Eddie says.

—I'm right here. The man takes a piece of soiled paper from his pocket. —Believe me, once you'd have known me clear as day.

The man seems to be in the shadows.

—Dark over there, Eddie says.

The man holds the paper near his good eye, squints, shakes his head, takes a magnifying glass from his pocket.

—Trouble with your eyes? Eddie says. Had trouble with mine as well.

—What? Yes. And how did it out?

—Cleared up completely.

—There we have it, the man says. He peers through the glass. —Completely? Just the thing. Let's see. It's a lot of crap. You've been appointed caretaker.

—Care?

—In recognition of your long-standing service, it says. You must be connected.

—How?

—Separate the useable material from the fill. You're certified here an expert.

—Certified expert?

—Me, too. You see me a messenger boy. Diminished capacity. But still hanging in, though I have my grievances. Bountiful grievances.

The man points to his feet.

Eddie looks at the man's running shoes. They are frayed and stained, bound with tape.

—My dear father, the man says, this was years ago, was a shoemaker. In those happy days, no self-respecting man would be seen outside his own home, the sacred domicile, in brightly colored cloth footgear, the likes of which might only be seen on women in certain quarters. Time was, a man's gear spoke a language: you got something, a cap, perhaps, of a peculiar and nonutilitarian design to speak your rank, and now—

Eddie nods. —All open to interpretation.

—No.

—Matters of opinion.

—A fact, the man says, is a fact.

—Cul, Eddie says, cul.

—Culturally determined paradigms of reality? Christ, don't pull that old saw on me.

—I don't want to pull anything, Eddie says.

—I had a message. I gave you the message. Will you stop this relentless, unbearable interrogation? What do you want from me? What more can you want from me?

—Well, Eddie says. I mean—

—Inadequate, the man says. Inadequate.

—All I want, Eddie says.

—All right, the man says. I have this job. My side of the fence. A monumental garden of memory. Valley of the Fallen. I watch to be sure no one disturbs it. All I could get, this. This, and they gave me some language.

.   .   .

Eddie finds a broken spade in a heap of burnt cans. He works from sunrise to sunset shoveling the styrofoam cups and plastic sheeting and paper and broken glass into piles. It is hopeless.

The full moon rises. Wolves and coyotes howl. Eddie needs a fire, but there is no wood on his side of the fence. On the other side, the sandy plain gives way to tree-covered hills.

Eddie goes over the fence, crawls across the plain, creeps up a hill. A voice whistles through the trees.

The security man stands surrounded by statuary in a dale. Eddie sees the flat, milky squares set in the turf.

—Look homeward, the man says. If it is here, it is everywhere, and the corollary applies as well.

Eddie thinks the man is talking to a sculpted soldier, but the man turns to a miniature granite house with lions guarding the entrance.

—Dark or light, the man says, it's all guilt. I get by. Nobody gives you anything. Make of it what you will. And you stones nodding. Always nodding. There's no escape. All theory aside.

The slabs are useable, and since Eddie cannot move them, he mounds fill at the slabs' bases and numbers the slabs with a bit of charred wood. He draws up a key.

There are some pieces, really quality material, that Eddie holds out. He uses a hard rock. Trial and error. Crude figurines. In time he learns the secret faults and the methodologies of flaking and shaping. He makes women. The forms are round, tending towards circularity. Squat, plump, round women.

The larger pieces, three-quarters lifesize, are made in

components and cemented together. Each piece is based on Dolores. Sometimes Eddie doubts his imagination. He sculpts her with the birds of the air. The birds form a circle at her feet, and some of the delicate creatures perch on her outstretched arms. Eddie is not sure if he has got it exactly right.

He spaces the pieces in a long oval: Dolores and the birds; eating at a table; pushing a broom; in ecstasy; at the beach; teaching a child; reading; to the centerpiece, where Dolores stands alone and serene in imagined moonlight; descending to Dolores burying the dead; drinking wine; smoking a cigarette; sleeping; walking in a garden; and rising from her bath, the water beading on her neck and breasts.

Eddie is almost finished when the security man comes back.

—This is it? the man says.

Eddie turns from his work. —Not quite done.

—I am, the man says.

—Finished?

—Papers came through today.

—Good?

—Best news in a hell of a while. The man lights a cigarette. —There it is. Imported. Saved this for a bit.

—Oh.

—All things in the fullness of time.

—Yeah.

—Every dog his moment in the sun.

—Think so?

—Hard work and perseverance. Deferred gratification. Don't teach that in the schools.

—No.

—I can see, the man says, from what you've done, that you're capable of work. Direction went a bit wrong, I'll grant that, but you'll be fine.

—Thanks.

—I have something for you.

Eddie follows him over the fence. A glen. Stream runs swiftly over rocks, foam building in the eddies. They walk a game trail to the water's edge.

—I remember, Eddie says, his eyes filling with tears, a place like this.

The man ducks under a bush. —Coming?

Eddie crawls after him. Small insects hover. Eddie inhales a few. He tries to keep the man in sight, but sweat runs into his eyes, and it is all flashes of light and the quick animal sounds of the man's forward motion.

A clearing.

—The old long haul, the man says.

Eddie gets up.

—Worth the effort. The man points.

A hut that looks like a cross between a geodesic dome and a yurt. The materials are eclectic—wooden beams, sheet metal, flattened cans, fiberboard, plastic sheeting, papier-mâché. Bracelets, necklaces, earrings, crucifixes, rings, beads, pictures, dolls, mirrors, bottles, rosaries, candlesticks, statues, etchings, and other objects hang from the shed. Parts of the hut shine brilliantly; other parts are dull and rotting.

—Very special thing, the man says, this.

—Where did it come from?

—Would you believe I built it, or that it's always been here? In one form or another.

Eddie chuckles politely.

—Well, it's yours now.

—Mine?

—Don't bother to thank me. The pleasure's in handing it on. Passing the torch.

—I, Eddie says.

—You'll be safe here. The man walks Eddie around the hut. —Each has its power. And what's underneath. Strong? It's solid.

Eddie looks through a window. The dirty glass has been lined with foil.

—If only my family had stayed.

—The foil, Eddie says.

—Fucking rays. The man gestures toward some beads and feathers. —Break up the patterns.

—Huh, Eddie says.

—Used to laugh at me. Theoretical. Now they're coming faster and faster. Through that widening hole. Experts agree.

—Good idea.

—I'd give you the keys, but there's no lock. Very safe out here. Far from the prying eye. The man unbuckles his pistol belt and hands it to Eddie. —Take this.

—You sure?

—Go ahead, open it.

Eddie unsnaps the holster. Instead of the regulation forty-five, there is a cheap twenty-five in oily wax paper.

—It's not original, Eddie says.

—You'll probably never use it. Just in case.

When the light starts to go, Eddie makes his way back to the clearing. Sleep comes easily.

He never disturbs the walls or floor or foil. The bones

of the Lost Kings have hardened and become encrusted with jewels. His statues are finished. He spends his days digging for the bones which will erase the past. Eddie finds buried things.

The sun gets to him. It seems that everything that has happened to him is happening. But nothing will affect him as long as he searches for the bones.

He wakes choking, crawls across the floor, outside. The woods are on fire. Heat waves shimmer above the trees. He stands. A light wind. The flames move toward the hut. Eddie sees a figure through the trees. Fritz ignites the woods with a flamethrower. The trenches Eddie has dug act as a firebreak.

—Shut it down, Eddie calls.

Fritz switches the thrower off. —What?

—You're going to burn my house.

—House? Fritz walks through the network of trenches to Eddie. He wears a black asbestos apron, and a welder's visor is tilted back on his head. —You have a house? A house that you own? Impossible.

Eddie points to the hut.

Fritz lights a cigarette and shakes his head. —This isn't in the plan.

—I live here.

—Off the charts, Fritz says.

—Since I fell by the wayside, Eddie says, it seems as though my voice has been drowned out. I talk and talk; it is, I think, a long scream, although no one seems to hear. Perhaps you think they don't hear because they have no interest in hearing a laundry list of gripes, but I think they do hear, as gibberish and nothing.

Fritz looks at his cigarette. —You want one of these?

—Please, Eddie says.

Fritz hands him a cigarette, gives him a light with a shiny Zippo. —Enjoy the break. Then I do the shack.

—You can't.

—Look at yourself, man. You had something once; now we find you howling like a dog on a chain.

—I should be destroyed, Eddie says. His right hand drifts to his side.

—Suit yourself, Fritz says.

Eddie takes the twenty-five from the holster, steps quick, jams the muzzle of the pistol under Fritz's chin. —Talk talk talk talk.

—We thought you were going to be a nice guy about this.

Eddie hears someone behind him. —Move and I'll blow his head off.

—Predictable, Fritz says.

—Nice trenches, the Businessman of the Saved says. From above, they form a sort of constellation. Bird or bear or something.

The Businessman of the Saved looks at the twenty-five. —Pretty puny. That thing won't protect you forever.

EDDIE: Just another minute.

B.O.S.: Ad infinitum?

EDDIE: Give me a chance to show what I can do.

B.O.S.: You're an ornament at best. Oh, don't pout. Lower the gun; I'll get you something.

Eddie gets the concession to the sculpture garden and the talisman hut. Fritz clears off the woods. The trenches are billed as ancient outerspace etchings. Eddie's statues are replaced with colorful fiberglass replicas. He will wear a blazer, slacks, tie. The company supplies the uniform, stocks the gift shop, provides a trailer.

The crowds are pretty good. Plump, sunburned families who stop for pictures: the kids climbing on the hut, Dad with his arm around Dolores as she rises from the bath. Local antiquaries with guidebooks. Teachers with their classes from the community college.

The visitors drop off. Blank pages in the guest book. Eddie never knows how much popcorn to pop or how many hot dogs to put in the roto-griller. The people who do come are strange. Women with thick accents and prayerbooks. Men clutching manuscripts. Two teenage boys with a telescope and sextant bring Eddie a case of Mexican beer. Eddie is forbidden to accept gratuities, but he takes the beer.

The Businessman of the Saved stops by. Eddie is showing the garden to a retired dentist. When the tour is finished, Eddie and the Businessman of the Saved walk.

B.O.S.: Sculpture gardens are white elephants.

EDDIE: What does it profit you to close?

B.O.S.: Sculpture, pit, it's all the same.

EDDIE: Pit?

B.O.S.: We made some power, we got some waste. Way of the world. We can't change it.

EDDIE: Power? Waste?

B.O.S.: Creates it. Law of nature. Nice idea, but it's out of my hands. We all have our limits.

EDDIE: I was commissioned.

B.O.S.: Assigned. Make-work proposition.

EDDIE: And?

B.O.S.: Hell of a headache, but it worked out. Turns out

to be a perfect storage site. Later, who knows? Maybe an aquarium. Or some kind of multiplex.

XII

A rig hauls Eddie's trailer to a wooded area far from the main gate. In Eddie's place they put up a cinderblock building. Eddie asks a workman what it is. The guy says it is a pumphouse. That is where Eddie hangs, waiting to see if they will have something for him. The security men will not let him inside. Eddie looks at himself on the closed-circuit monitor at the checkpoint. They give him an application and lend him a ballpoint and correction fluid. He has a problem with the address blank. He puts *on site*. Position desired: *any*.

The security chief looks at Eddie's form.

—You think they'll have something?

The man shrugs.

—When will I hear?

—Thank you for your interest in the firm.

Eddie waits each day. The security men ignore him. Some of the other employees say hello. Eddie takes their cordiality as a good sign. The employees are well-dressed. Eddie knows he must dress as who he wants to be. He makes sure to put on his necktie, and he never carries a lunch. Someday he will get an umbrella and carry that. He waits in the heat of the day by the soda machine.

A woman in labcoat and eyeglasses talks to Eddie. She works in the pumphouse.

—Running the pumps? Eddie says.

—Not like you think.

—Oh, Eddie says, I understand.

—It's all monitored.

—Yes, yes.

—Electronically, you know, by computers.

—You watch the computers?

—The graphics. On a screen.

—If the pump breaks, you fix it? Or the pipes? You know how to fix pipes?

—The crews do that.

—So, Eddie says, so to get in, I don't have to know how to fix pumps or pipes?

—It depends on your classification.

—Yeah.

—There are different jobs.

—I understand, Eddie says.

—Don't give up, the woman says.

At night, Eddie thinks about the pumphouse. Not what the name implies, he knows. He pictured the place as a damp, dark area crisscrossed with pipes, valves, gauges, catwalks. Now he knows it is cool and clean. Fluorescent lighting. Quiet. The technicians sit at their desks, watching the screens. Colored lines trace the water's progress through the system. The network of pipes and pumps is buried deep underground in bunker-like tunnels.

The head guard comes to the soda machine. —This is not helping you.

—I'm ready and available, Eddie says.

—I sent your paper along. Takes time to go through channels. You will be contacted.

—I know that.

—You got to get out of here. The guard hands Eddie a ticket. —Go down front and take the tour.

The central administrative complex is really something: a thirty-story glass-and-steel octagon with neo-something cornices and archways and a giant clock set at the apex. Inside, gloved Courtesy Girls greet the tourists and offer tea, cookies, towelettes. The offices are large and airy with simulated wood floors so durable, the guide says, they could not be damaged with a blowtorch. There are Oriental carpets and wet bars and streamlined desks and copier rooms and departments: Sales, Training, Documentation, Promotion, Internal Communications, Security, Production, Human Resources, and many more.

The grounds are even better. There are brooks and organic sculptures and stone benches and alabaster cherubs and goddesses and groves of fruit trees and reflecting pools and rock gardens.

A man in coveralls prunes a pear tree.

—Funny, Eddie says.

—What?

—You trim artificial trees?

—They're real.

Eddie looks around. —Doesn't it freeze in the winter?

—No, not when controlled with climate-sensitive implants and micro-botanical pumps. The chips tell them how to grow.

Eddie moves along, takes in the storage silos, car pools, heavy-equipment sheds, independent installations. He likes the cooling pools, the long azure rectangles that recall postcard canals.

.   .   .

Word is Eddie better keep away from the pumphouse.
There is a time for retrenchment. Eddie stays in the trailer
and writes long letters to whom it may concern, stating
the facts of his case. Although he knows he must go to the
top, Eddie does not want to seem unreasonable. He states
his preference for a slot in the pumphouse. Any position
will do. But he is careful to indicate that he understands
such a plum may not immediately come his way. Eddie
suggests that some of the free space on-site could be used
as a civic center where athletes and other performers
could put on spectacular programs of entertainment. This
would not only increase civic feeling, it would also create
jobs, permanent employment for ushers, concession-stand
workers, cleaning people, etc.

He waits when the shifts change and catches the workers.
He holds the sheaf of letters like a stack of pamphlets.
Most employees pass without looking at him, but a few
politely accept the blotted sheets of notebook paper.

The woman emerges from the crowd. —I wondered
what happened to you.

—Still here, Eddie says. They won't dislodge me.

—That's good.

—Determination is half the battle, Eddie says. Well,
determination and enthusiasm.

—I see.

—You can't rule out enthusiasm, Eddie says.

—Great attitude, the woman says.

—I visualize myself a success, Eddie says. I think it's
really helping. Every day, I feel better and better.

.   .   .

Someone pounds on the trailer's door. Eddie jumps up. His first impulse is to go for a weapon. —Coming, he says. Just a minute.

He opens the door.

Fritz stands on the cinderblock that serves as a stoop.

—You? Eddie says.

—Let me in, Fritz says.

Eddie stands aside.

—Nice, Fritz says. He folds the converted bed into the wall, pulls out the legs, and it becomes the dining table. —Seen worse. Shit, lived in worse.

—What do you want?

—They asked me to talk to you. Your letter went up the chain. Now you got results.

—Which one?

Fritz shrugs. —Who knows? Your plea's been heard, right? That's what you wanted, right? Sometimes, frankly, I wonder about the clarity of people's objectives. Read any of those books about how to prioritize?

—Books?

—Doesn't matter. Check your TV set. They have these people on periodically. I know what you want— you want to get inside. Everybody wants inside—hell, you need to cling to something.

—No problem, Eddie says.

—But these letters, Fritz says, this out there thing, this here-I-am-world. I don't think so. If you're a nut case and you want attention, okay, you got it. But I hate to let it go that way for you.

—What I want, Eddie says, is to show what I can do.

—We're fully aware of what you're capable of. By the way, are you in the possession of any firearms?

—Of course not.

—I want you to think of me as a friend, Fritz says. But to be honest with you, pal, you are barking up the wrong tree. You got some coffee or something?

—Instant okay?

—My favorite.

Eddie pops two mugs of water in the microwave.

—I understand, Fritz says. I've been where you're at.

—Uh huh, Eddie says.

He spoons the crystals into the mugs, stirs, hands a mug to Fritz, and waits to hear more.

Someone shoves a letter under the door of Eddie's trailer. It says he is to report to Central Administration so he can be a member of the floating pool. Eddie reports. He is given white paint, pans, rollers.

—When you've covered that one, see me, the supervisor says. I'll have something else for you.

They follow a concrete path to the orchards. Eddie steers the woman from the pumphouse onto a woodchip-covered trail that leads to a moon-viewing platform overlooking a rock garden. The air is heavy with the sweet perfume of ripening fruit. Golden mechanical birds sing unearthly melodies in the trees. Colors swirl in the half light. Lemons and oranges are imbued with sensual flesh tones, cherries and plums take on deep and rich hues. Eddie notices the iridescent sheen of the woman's black dress, the heavy, smooth sway of her movements. As they begin the ascent to the viewing platform, he reaches for her hand. It flutters like a tiny bird until it rests securely in the steely trap of Eddie's grasp.

She lets out a low moan. —Oh, God.

Eddie strokes her hair, guides her to a bench. The moon shines over the rock garden.

—Marry me, Eddie gasps.

XIII

Things pick up at work. Eddie goes to the head of the department, a young woman named Linda.

—What can you do? Linda says.

—Hmm, Eddie says.

—In terms of the department?

Eddie puts his best foot forward.

Linda smiles vaguely, nods. —Impressive. Unfortunately, we have a staff of much more qualified people. No reflection on you; it's just that we have so many exceptional candidates.

—I understand.

—I'll give you what I can.

—You won't regret it. I need the work, and I'll work hard. I'm thinking of starting a family.

They give him a selection of brushes and six colors in an oil-based product he has never used.

—Two things, the supervisor says. Get the slogan in, and give the finished product a few coats of varnish. That's for your durability.

Eddie nods and carries his equipment up the ladder to the billboard. He does a brilliant sky, fluffy clouds, radiant sun, and arcs the words AQUARIUM OF THE FUTURE across it. Eddie works in hills with neatly shaped cypress trees. Although he has not seen the plans, he paints the aquarium as a giant swimming pool with three concrete walls and a glass front. Fish, squid, sharks, and barracudas contend in the water. The picture is glossy, professionally done. Still, a bit cold. Needs something. He puts a brontosaurus in the water. Pterodactyls fly overhead. A mastodon grazes on a hillside.

A secretary shows him into the office. Eddie slumps in the chair and says he will have coffee. It is all over. There are studies of canals on the walls. To be built with the future in mind. Now that he is X'd out, Eddie feels pain and guilt and loss. Opportunities, he sees, were placed before him on a silver platter, but he never capitalized on them because he lived his life wrong, with no direction or thought. Now the canals will be built without him, and who can say what green and pleasant land will spring forth here?

A man in a suit comes in.

Eddie rises.

—Don't get up. The man shakes Eddie's hand. —Sorry I'm late. He looks at Eddie's coffee cup. —I see you've been taken care of. Good. There's a trend nowadays to refuse all offered beverages. Frankly, I don't like this trend one bit.

Eddie slumps back in his chair.

—In China, for example, somebody wants to talk business, what's he offer you?

—I don't know, Eddie says.

—Cup of tea and a cigarette. You think you refuse either one? Not if you want to do business.

—What have you got to lose? Eddie says.

The man chuckles. —Indeed. He opens a manila folder. —You've intersected with some of our top people. Very impressive.

—Thanks.

—May I speak off the record?

Eddie nods.

—I've received a call or calls on your behalf from a certain party or parties.

—Great.

—Great, and not so great. We like to think a clearly defined chain of command is the hallmark of an efficient operation. And we are an efficient operation.

—Yeah?

—The kind of immediate access you are used to is a thing of the past. Bottom line: We're a joint governmental/private sector initiative with a specific mission. Can you see yourself fitting into that sort of structure?

—Sure, Eddie says. In fact, I've got some ideas. I've been doing the billboards—designing a logo, really, like a basic model, but I think I could expand on it. Put some people in the picture, some world leaders maybe, and some women, and a dog. Something that'll catch on. Then kick it—on T-shirts, coffee mugs, posters—you know. Push it and push it. Push as hard as the market will bear. That's success. Do you agree?

The form says Eddie is in the Promotions Department, but he has to report to the gym. A towel boy tells him the trainer is busy teaching low-impact aerobics. Eddie has a look around. Basketball court with a well-surfaced track running around the upper level, weight rooms with computer-assisted machines, Olympic pool, saunas, locker rooms. He keeps his eyes open for heavy and speed bags. Eddie cannot find any.

—You are the guy Mr. Thompson called about? the trainer says.

—I guess. Eddie follows the man into an office.

—What I see, the trainer says, is low body fat, but equally low muscle mass. Skinny. You smoke?

—Need one?

—Quit. You'll need lung capacity. Drink?

—Well . . .

—Quit. The trainer gives Eddie a pamphlet. —Follow the diet and use a multi-vitamin. Run. Two miles a day. Build up to ten. Strength is the big problem.

—I may not look like much, Eddie says, but I can handle myself in a pinch.

—Yeah, yeah, the trainer says.

Eddie trains hard. The work pays off. He breathes easier. His troubles are gone. The running is nothing. Eddie feels strong as a bull.

The day of the shoot they treat him like a king. Beautiful women approach offering food and drink. Eddie looks at their hair and athletic suits and does not know what to say. There are cables and cameras, generators and lights, even a small crane.

Thompson greets Eddie. —You know what we need. Just swim the canal. Don't worry about the rest.

—Yeah, Eddie says, I got it.

—Just jump in the water and swim.

—Okay. There's one thing, though, I have my doubts about. A little problem.

Thompson stiffens. —Doubts, no.

—More of a question, really.

—Fine. Whatever you need to know.

—It's only a hundred yards?

—Good question. We welcome questions, particularly good ones like yours.

A whistle blows.

—You have to go, man.

Eddie walks to the edge of the canal. Two production assistants slip the robe from his body. The trainer massages his shoulders and neck, whispers in his ear.

Eddie stands at the edge.

Dives.

XIV

Eddie and Deirdre are married in the company chapel. Mr. Thompson and Mr. Thompson's lovely wife, Mrs. Thompson, serve as witnesses. There is a small reception in the basement of the chapel. Most of those in attendance are friends of the bride. Mr. Thompson presents Eddie with some envelopes that acquaintances in the firm have sent. Eddie puts them in his jacket for later.

Deirdre would like a honeymoon in Paris or Rome. Eddie favors the Yucatán or Tahiti. This is not to be. The newlyweds are needed at work. Mr. Thompson has booked them a honeymoon suite at a suburban hotel. It is the least he can do, Mr. Thompson says.

Best of all is the house, a brand new two-bedroom in the company development, Garden Groves. Eddie and Deirdre are able to get it with almost nothing down through a special program. The rate is very favorable, and the payments are deducted from their wages.

Eddie and Deirdre go out to look the place over. Eddie determines the construction is sound. The living room is done in faux Chippendale, the dining room has a sturdy walnut table and captain's chairs, the kitchen appliances are energy-efficient. It is all perfect.

In the bedroom, Deirdre is sprawled on the fourposter bed. Eddie sits in the country French rocker.

—Come here, Deirdre says. I have something for you.

Deirdre takes him by the hand and leads him downstairs, down another flight to the basement. There are a laundry area and a storeroom and a room that is refinished as a den with a roll-top desk, Victorian couch, bookcases, and antique globe.

—All this, Eddie says, his voice trembling.

Happy are their days. At work, Deirdre is promoted, although Eddie is not sure what she is promoted to. It is technical. Eddie is made swimmaster at the aquarium, just as Mr. Thompson promised he would be. The dolphins and killer whales arrive with specially trained special trainers, another married couple. They are handsome people—blond and tan in their neoprene wetsuits. They run the spectacles and swims they erroneously call fish shows. Everyone knows dolphins and killer whales are aquatic mammals, as Eddie is tempted to point out. But it is not too bad. Eddie has an athletic suit and cap with his title on them and a chrome whistle and expensive-looking plastic sandals. He carries a clipboard and makes sure no one is in danger and no one drowns.

He stops at the Humane Society after work. More variety than he expected. Tiers of steel cages, concrete floor with drain, the smell of animals and feed. Eddie grabs a puppy and signs the papers. An attendant puts the dog in a box that folds shut. Deirdre loves the puppy from the moment she opens the box. She rushes out to get it food and dog bowls and chew bones and toys and a cedar-filled pet bed.

—What's he called? Deirdre says.

—You decide, Eddie says.

Each evening, as they lie entwined in each other's arms in the fourposter, Deirdre says, Bobby, or Henry, or Herman, or Jesse, or Frank.

Eddie says, it is up to you.

Eddie converts the storage room to a home workshop. He makes a pegboard holder and hangs his newly purchased tools from it. He buys a workbench kit and assembles it. When the bench is finished, Eddie stains the raw pine a rich color and bolts a big metal vise to it.

His first real project is building a house for the dog. Eddie gets the plans from a magazine and goes to the lumber yard for plywood, screws, nails, tarpaper, glue.

The doghouse takes no time. Eddie places it at the base of one of the clothespoles and steps back to admire his work. The shiny rows of nailheads gleam on the tarpaper roof. The dog sniffs the house, barks, runs away. Deirdre calls and whistles, tells the dog he is a good boy, tries to coax him into the doghouse. The dog sits looking at Deirdre, his tongue hanging out of his mouth.

—He needs to get used to it, Eddie says.

Eddie steps behind the dog and grabs its collar. He pulls the dog to its feet and tries to drag it to the doghouse. The dog snarls, twists his head, snaps at Eddie's wrist.

Calls start coming at all hours of the night. The princess phone rings. Eddie reaches over and grabs it.

—Will you shut that dog up? a man says. He is keeping my kids awake.

—Okay, Eddie says.

The calls come every night. When Eddie tries to tell the caller that it must be another dog, the caller shouts obscenities and threatens to telephone the authorities.

Eddie stops after work and gets a big, heavy muzzle. He takes the muzzle out of the bag. Deirdre backs away.

A dark figure with a long gun runs across the lawn. Deirdre screams. The figure turns and fires. Eddie dives, forces Deirdre down onto the grass. A second gunman somewhere. Eddie observes the graceful arc of tracer fire against the dark suburban sky. He tries to shield Deirdre. But Deirdre wriggles out from under him. Eddie reaches for her wrist but catches the knife blade instead. Deirdre pulls away, leaving Eddie with a long gash across the palm of his hand. He sees her lunge at the dark figure. The figure fires and Deirdre goes down. Eddie rolls to the doghouse and fires from behind it. The figure stumbles, drops the long gun, pulls out a short one. Eddie hears another gun. Eddie's ammo runs out. The sun comes up. Automatic lawn sprinklers come on.

XV

An extraordinarily bright day, the day of Deirdre's funeral, and the glare bothers Eddie. Everything—the shiny hearse and limousines, the marble tombstones, the hard, cloudless sky, even the nitrogen-enriched grass—reflects some terrible light and leaves Eddie feeling dull and weak. Some kind of minister stands at the graveside. Their marriage was so short, their time together so sweet and fleeting, he never asked her religious affiliation, if any.

When the glare is too much, Eddie closes his eyes. He

could faint, but Eddie does not feel faint. People do faint, he knows. Perfectly normal. A sign of strong emotion or even identification. Not for him. Eddie opens his eyes. The minister closes his book.

People drift away. Some pause to shake Eddie's hand and murmur a few words of solace. Eddie knows what to do. He nods and softly says *thank you.* Mr. Thompson comes over, hand outstretched.

—Terrible thing, Mr. Thompson says.

—Thank you, Eddie says.

—Don't worry. It's all buried. Nobody will ever know.

—Know?

—You are safe. Garden Groves is coming down.

—Thank you, Eddie says.

—All on a toxic dump. Bulldoze it and let her sit for a while. Monitor the site.

—That's a great comfort to me, Eddie says.

—Put up something else. After she cools down. You may be able to help.

Eddie nods solemnly and greets other mourners until someone ushers him to a car.

The car brings Eddie to company headquarters. Two men in dark suits greet him and take him to a room in the basement: a table and three wooden chairs.

—Sit, one man says.

The other man drops a package of cigarettes and a book of matches on the table. —Go ahead.

Eddie opens the pack and takes a cigarette.

—Comfortable?

Eddie nods.

—All right. The man straddles one of the chairs.

The other man sits facing Eddie. —Let's get going. I'm Bob, and this is Jim. We're your friends in the company. Your legal advisors, you might say.

They interrogate Eddie for twenty hours.

Eddie is given a small room with a single bed, dresser, and sink. The toilet and shower stalls are down the hall. A woman brings him food in styrofoam trays.

Everything is explained. Eddie cannot go home. The house is sealed. It may be best not to see the place again. Put the past behind him. The company gives him a small settlement for his possessions and equity.

Eddie has no duties; the company is giving him some time for readjustment. He spends his days in the lounge at the end of the hall, watching television.

A game show is on when Mr. Thompson comes in. —I tried your room.

Eddie turns off the TV. —Just killing time.

—Climbing the walls, huh? Mr. Thompson hands Eddie a shopping bag. —I brought you a few things.

Eddie nods and looks in the bag: razor, toothbrush, cigarettes, lighter, and other items. Eddie weeps. He sobs. His shoulders shake. His nose runs.

—Easy, Mr. Thompson says. Now, now.

—Thank you. Thank you so much.

—Not at all. Now get a hold of yourself.

Eddie shakes his head. —It's too late.

—Be a man. I hate to say it, but that's what it comes down to. In the end, that's all there is.

—For what? What does it profit me?

—You can't go on like this.

Eddie clutches his head. —My world is dark. Dark.

—We must go on. Terrible thing that happened. And other things, believe it or not, just as terrible. Happening now. Or yet to happen.

—You see, Eddie says.

—I try to remember, Mr. Thompson says, that we will all die just as dead as the dead are now, someday.

—Does it help? Eddie weeps harder.

Mr. Thompson takes the handkerchief from his pocket. —Take it. I think you need something. Maybe a raise.

—Can hold me, Eddie says, but it's coming. Believe me, it is coming.

Mr. Thompson backhands Eddie so hard that Eddie is knocked halfway out of his chair. —You're a lucky man.

—Lucky?

—You are not at the bottom. Nowhere close. In fact, you're nearer the top. Take a look down there; it's hell.

Eddie wipes his face with the handkerchief.

—We need to get you back in the swing of things. My wife has a sister who's recently divorced . . .

Eddie works in an office coding documents. The work is simple, matching up numbers, mostly, but it requires a dogged concentration. When he is able to surrender completely to the numbers, he finds peace. Eddie thanks Mr. Thompson for the work.

He begins to watch his coworkers. And then to make a few notes. The notes grow into dossiers. He keeps the dossiers in his room, hidden, to the extent they can be, in the closet. None of the subjects is identified by name in the dossiers; Eddie assigns them numbers.

People are not fools. They will not jeopardize their livelihoods by committing major infractions at work. Performance is the last thing to go. But there is hearsay. People talk a great deal, and the talk in the department is very loose indeed.

It is the private things, the private, sexual things, that most interest Eddie.

—You need to get out, Mr. Thompson says.

Sunday. They are in the lounge. Eddie is watching a program about cookware.

—Out?

—You look blue.

—Blue?

—Green around the gills.

—I don't feel—

—You've been cooped up too long.

—I'm not sure.

—A supervised visit.

Mr. Thompson drives. Eddie lies blindfolded on the floor in back. Mr. Thompson warns him repeatedly not to get up or make unnecessary movement.

Eddie groans. His knees are drawn up to his chest, and the car turns again and again.

The car stops. Eddie hears a door slam. Mr. Thompson opens the back door. —Sit up. Open your eyes slowly; you'll get used to the light.

Eddie tries to roll up into a ball. Mr. Thompson is surprisingly strong. He forces Eddie up on the back seat.

—Let go, Eddie says.

Mr. Thompson slaps him. —Quit whining, baby.

Eddie opens his mouth.

Mr. Thompson hits him again.

.   .   .

The store is bright. Eddie stumbles and slides.

Mr. Thompson takes him by the arm. —Sorry about the rough stuff.

—Don't mention it.

—Let Deirdre go.

—Please, Eddie says, never speak her name.

—I understand. Mr. Thompson takes a list from inside his jacket. —I'll let you shop around.

Eddie wanders through the aisles. He looks at rows of work boots, drifts through housewares to sporting goods. The guns are locked in glass cabinets. The ammunition is in a case behind the counter. A young man sells some bullets to an elderly woman and steps over to the gun cabinet to show her a bolt action twenty-two rifle. Eddie leans on the counter. The ammunition cabinet is still open, glass door slid away, keys dangling in the stainless lock. Eddie steps quickly behind the counter and grabs a box of .25 ACP rounds. The clerk is showing the woman how to remove the bolt from the rifle. Eddie opens the box, spills cartridges onto the floor. The clerk looks.

Eddie crouches and begins picking up the cartridges. —Sorry. I was trying to see if these were the right kind.

—I'll take care of it, the clerk says.

Eddie puts the box on the counter.

Eddie knows his room has been searched. The files are intact. He wonders if the searchers copied the dossiers.

—We have a project for you, Mr. Thompson says. Posters. We are quite excited about this. These posters will go out in schools to the young people. The company feels

that by giving young people posters with positive messages—well, you know, the benefits are obvious.

A small, windowless room on a lower level. Drafting table,
chair, wastebasket, art supplies. No phone. Eddie works on
some sketches. He has some idea what they want. Drugs,
for example. The bad side. That is the point, Eddie thinks,
of education, to make the bad side so clear, so true-to-life,
that there can be no doubt what is out there waiting for you.

Eddie looks through the dusty sketches in the OUT box. All
wrong. Days pass. Eddie works, the floor of the office
ankle-deep in rejected studies, until he gets a poster right:
an angular, idealized nude couple locked in a passionate
embrace beneath the legend PEOPLE NEED TO BREED.

Mr. Thompson sits at the drafting table. —Hello.
    —Hello.
    —Saw your picture, Ed.
    —And?
    —We have a little problem.
    —No.
    —A misunderstanding. Mr. Thompson gets up and
walks around the room. —What is the story behind this?
    —There isn't any story, Eddie says.
    —We expected a more traditional approach. The vir-
tues of civic virtue, something like that. But there's no
story, right? You said that. You just said there is no story
here. No story whatsoever, correct?
    —Well—
    —I'll get the story. The story will come out. They'll get
you in a room and tell you the story.

—If that's the way it is, Eddie says.

—I saw a program on TV, Mr. Thompson says, about some happy people. They worked hard and they played hard. Why? Because they knew how to live.

Bob and Jim take Eddie to an interrogation room. A mirror on one wall.

—Why don't you give it to us again, Jim says.

—I told you, Eddie says. Told you it all.

—Tell him one more time, Bob says.

—I can't talk about it, Eddie says.

—Scary, huh? Bob says.

—You know what's scary, Jim says, is people in cars. You're in a parking ramp or walking down the street, and you see these people sitting in cars. Not doing anything. Watching. Watching for what, you have to think.

—We have had some reports, Bob says.

—These things come in threes, Jim says. Tell us everything you know.

—What are your dreams? Bob says.

—A little house with a subcompact in front? Jim says.

Bob laughs. —Can't have been much of a life in Garden Groves with—

Eddie stands up. —Don't speak their names.

—Easy, Jim says. We live in town. Fashionable area. What films do you see?

—Mooooovies? Bob says.

—Quit the fucking routine, Eddie says.

—And do what? Jim says. Talk about the weather? Sporting events? Maybe the economy? We know you too well for that. Since we're alone here, I could tell you the story of my life. My childhood, that unhappy, cramped house, the experiences that formed me. The deaths of my pets. The cruelties of my family. The sense that we were missing out on something, not just the new cars and wall-to-wall carpeting and boats and ponies and swimming pools and motor bikes, but some human reality whose absence left me hurt and empty. We could begin with my earliest memory, the sunlight in the garden, and work through every hurt and slight to the dysfunction and nigh inevitable breakup of the family.

—Nothing, Bob says, is more boring than other people's stories.

The wall around the mirror swings open. Mr. Thompson walks in. —Hold it right there.

Eddie starts to cough. He wheezes, bends over in his chair.

—Things seem to have gotten off track, Mr. Thompson says. You've lost your focus.

Eddie takes the pistol out of his sock. He sits straight up, says, —Blip, blip, blip—and fires three times.

Bob and Jim are each hit in the chest. Mr. Thompson is shot through his open mouth.

—Terrible thing, Eddie says, terrible thing.

XVI

Eddie flies over the interstate in a giant Oldsmobile. The pressure is off. He has the car and nine hundred dollars.

Eddie will bury the past. He will burn the car across the country. Head south where it is warm all the time. Lose the Olds in a swamp.

Now it is fast food from the drive-thrus, and beer and ice and cigarettes when he stops for fuel. A styrofoam cooler rides on the back seat.

Eddie will settle in a city on the coast. Get a place near

the water. Work. A job where people do not ask questions. Not much. Place, job, life. Pure and simple.

He is plagued by memories. Dreams. He leaves the lights on when he sleeps. He wakes in strange motels. Eddie jumps up, runs to the bathroom, splashes water on his face. He trembles a bit. But it stops after a while.

Eddie drives over long, flat stretches. His mind wanders. He sees himself in the future with a happy home. A companion. Soul mate. A happy family.

Eddie catches himself. —Wake up, he says. He fears he may not be able to stay awake.

His thoughts are nothing. Eddie keeps his pistol handy.

Usually, he catches the last billboarded motel before the chains, but before he knows it, he is downtown. Eddie crosses the city, finds a place on the far side of the beltway.

He is being followed. Three men in a luxury sedan. The men wear suits. Their haircuts are neat; their ties are knotted. Businessmen. Awake and aware. Going about their business. Working. Watching.

Eddie exits at a tourist court with an arctic motif— each cabin a mock igloo. The sedan stays on the freeway.

Nerves.

They are after him. In threes or twos or ones. As many as grains of sand on a beach. Two in a Volvo outside the igloo. Three in a cargo van across a flat state.

Eddie sweats in the lunch line of a fried chicken drive-thru, ten-dollar bill in one hand, his twenty-five in the other. He is boxed. They could blip him clean. Man steps around the corner of the building, sprays and prays, Eddie is waxed. He should have thought.

Nobody comes around. The food smells good. Moist fat seeps through the bottom of the cardboard box. Eddie swings the car around and heads north.

No more drive-thrus. He fills a thermal mug with coffee at gas stations. Throws ice water from the cooler in his face when he is about to drop off.

Eddie heads for the neighborhoods he knew best. His hair has grown long and unkempt; Eddie ties it back with a strip of motel towel. He cleans his pistol with his toothbrush, carves the letter D in the wooden stock, keeps the weapon in the pocket of his work shirt.

He thinks he remembers a place where everything lost is found. Or where something was lost. Or the king lived there. He cannot keep it straight. But there is a place. Places cannot disappear. There is a law to that effect, a law of nature.

There is a wide avenue: strip mall on one side, fast food outlets on the other. Beyond the plastic roofs, a subdivision stretches over gently rolling hills. Swimming pools sparkle like gems in the sunset.

Eddie stops at a pizza place. He has to wait for a table. The families in the lobby are neat. They have straight white teeth. Eddie is embarrassed. More families crowd in behind him. He looks at some fliers on the wall.

Eddie sees the face, grainy and aged, bloated on the shoddy bill for self-defense training, glaring out above the address and phone number.

Eddie knocks. The house is an aluminum-sided rambler with attached garage.

The door swings open.

—What can I do you for? Fritz says. He stiffens and his right hand shoots out.

Eddie jumps back, lands in a defensive posture.

—Huh, Fritz says, afraid of your own shadow?

Eddie steps forward and sticks out his hand.

Fritz takes it. —Guess we all are, on closer examination. How the hell are you?

—Okay, Eddie says. Okay.

Fritz leads Eddie into the living room. Eddie sits down on a plastic-covered recliner.

—Angela, Fritz calls, c'mere. Grab a couple brewskies.

A middle-aged blonde woman comes in with two cans of beer. She wears a house dress and apron.

—Here's the ball-and-chain, Fritz says. I mean the better half. Just kiddin' you, honey.

Eddie stands up. The plastic chair cover crinkles.

Angela hands him a beer. —Hi.

—Hello, Eddie says, pleased to meet you.

—Ed, here, Fritz says, is an old pal of mine. Comrade in arms, you might put it.

—Oh. Angela turns and goes back to the kitchen.

—Nice home, Eddie calls after her.

They walk after dinner.

—Good for you, Fritz says, patting his beer gut. —Work off a little of this.

Eddie nods and takes the cigar Fritz offers him. Fritz leads Eddie to a small rise and points out the water tower, high school, mall. Eddie looks out over the terrain. He had remembered it as flat, not gently rolling.

Fritz points to a house. —My boy lives there. Down there at the mall, we got some quiet interests down there.

—You really made something of yourself.

—Hell, it could all have been yours. Fritz relights his cigar. —Look. Look and you see. I paid my dues.

—And me?

—The past is the past, Fritz says. Nobody wants it back.

—Can't get it back, Eddie says.

—Don't look so pure, Fritz says. There's that thing, that thing you made small, but it's still there. Could come back on you. Unless you do right, you know?

XVII

Fritz has a rec room with a wet bar in the basement, and he throws a drinking party. His boy is there, and Eddie, men from the subdivision, friends from the firm. Eddie sits on a ladder-back barstool, drinking draft from the beermeister. Fritz works the bar in his NAME YOUR POISON apron. Later, they will show adult videos on the wide screen TV. Now a football game is going. Eddie cannot see the screen. Fritz puts popcorn in front of him.

A beefy man called the Colonel tells about his days in the firm. The others laugh.

—You remember, Fritz? the Colonel says. Christ, I don't know how we did it. You remember that one?

—That one and many more, Fritz says. He is drinking iced gin from a water tumbler, and his face is flushed. —Christ, if we had time to go over all the stunts we pulled. Fritz fills a plastic pitcher from the beermeister and places it in front of Eddie. —Cheer up, sad sack.

Eddie nods weakly.

—Grim one, the Colonel says. What's to be grim about? We're all friends here.

Eddie nods again.

—Trying to bring us down? the Colonel says.

—Easy, Fritz says. How about a fresh drink?

—I'm easy, the Colonel says. Just asking a question. An easy question at that.

—Huh, Eddie says.

—It's not like I'm going to stand him on his fucking head, the Colonel says.

—Our friend, here, suffered a loss, Fritz says. His wife and dog, home and family—

Eddie bends down his head and cries.

—Is he sick? Fritz's boy says.

—Don't, Eddie says, ever speak their names.

—I get you, Fritz says.

—No names, the Colonel says. He's that much sense at least. At first, I wasn't sure.

—How about another, Colonel? Fritz says. Another story of the battles we've won.

The Colonel and Fritz laugh. Fritz walks from behind the bar and throws his arm around the Colonel.

They sing:

> The damage I've done,
> And the battles I've won,
> The past I'll disclose,
> And the secrets I'll enclose,
> We've had troubles and guns,
> Now the dirty deed's done,
> And my love for you, dear, has just begun.

Fritz goes up on tiptoe for the last line, stumbles. The Colonel catches him. The guests applaud and whistle. Fritz sits on a stool next to Eddie.

—I got a rich one, he says. Tell me, Ed, are you familiar with the boxer in the cage?

Eddie grunts.

The Colonel shakes his head.

—We had this philosophy professor, Fritz says. From a major university, yet. How the hell he ended up in our hands, who knows? This was the old detention center, with cages where the guards walked overhead on catwalks. Foreign design. Called them tiger cages. So the professor goes in the cage. Fat, lazy bastard with spectacles. We figured he'd go nuts without his books. At first it looked that way, but then he started to work out. Shadow box. He'd box and box and run in place and do push-ups and so forth, all fucking day, every fucking day. And it worked. Old fatty trimmed down and muscled up, but it affected his mind as well. They call him out of the cage, and he won't budge. Won't answer to his name. Insists he's a fighter. So Stan Leary goes in after him, and sure enough, he breaks Stan's jaw in three places with a left hook.

The Colonel laughs.

Eddie puts his head down on the bar.

—Of course, Fritz says, we had to shoot him.

—How about that movie? the Colonel says.

—Soon enough, Fritz says. We haven't finished the preliminaries. He reaches over the bar and gets a deck of cards. —Little three-hand, eh, boys? He elbows Eddie in the ribs. —How about whippin' the old third hand out?

The Colonel sits on the other side of Eddie. Fritz deals each of the men three cards, face down. Eddie tosses off a mug of beer, then another.

—Who was at the house that night? Eddie says.

—Like I know, Fritz says.

—Like anybody knows anything, the Colonel says. He snaps his fingers.

Fritz's boy comes down the bar and refills Fritz's and the Colonel's drinks.

—So I'm psychic, Fritz says.

—A fortune-teller, the Colonel says.

—Shut up and flip over the cards, Eddie says.

Eddie has three queens, each depicted by a nude woman. The queens of hearts and diamonds look familiar. The queen of spades has black tape over her eyes.

—Imported, Fritz says. Scandinavian, get me?

—Turn them up, Eddie says. Turn it fucking over.

—In a nutshell, Fritz says.

The Colonel laughs. —Which one is it under?

—Practice hand, Fritz says. He scoops up the cards. —I'll deal the fair deal of the just.

Eddie lurches toward Fritz.

The Colonel pulls Eddie back. —Sing us a song.

—Gimme a drink, Eddie says.

—Song first, the Colonel says.

Eddie stands on his bar stool and sings:

Looking out o'er the brim o' me gimme cap,
I see the world and the sun shining bright.
It shines through the day and on through the night,
It burns through my eyes, Lord it's too fucking bright.
It burns and it burns to the back of my skull,
And some days I ask myself if I'm doing well.

Eddie sways, changes tunes, and rasps out:

Drink your whiskey, drink your gin,
Don't be afraid of anythin',

Forget the old lady and original sin,
Down the whiskey, finish the gin.

He clambers down from the stool.

—Wa aah aah, Eddie says. He coughs, doubles over.

The Colonel strikes him sharply on the back. —Quite a performance. Ought to take a prize.

Eddie straightens up, panting.

—What could we award our friend? Fritz says.

The Colonel takes a trucker's wallet from inside his coat. —Damn, I'm a bit short.

—Don't be vulgar, Fritz says. It should be something more personal. What would you like?

—Like? Eddie says. I'd like to be—no, that's stupid. He takes a gulp of beer.

—No, the Colonel says. Tell us what you want.

—Let it go by, Eddie says.

—Maybe a rubber suit, Fritz says, with a crest on it? A trophy? Loving cup for public display?

—I had it all, Eddie says.

—Have you, now? the Colonel says. Well, pardon our fucking offerings. Obviously, they're trinkets to a man like yourself, a man who knows it all.

—Hey, Fritz shouts, let's put the movie in. Freshen up the drinks, boys, and grab an extra. This picture is guaranteed to wet your whistles.

Fritz's boy fiddles with the VCR. The men drag chairs and stools to the TV. Eddie stays at the bar.

—Come along, friend, the Colonel says. This will perk you up. Love, eh? Amore, get me?

—Uh huh, Eddie says. He goes behind the bar to fill his pitcher. —I'll be along.

—Pulling that, the Colonel says. I never thought you'd pull that on us. And at a party.

Fritz walks over from the TV. —Come on, fellas. You'll miss the matinée.

—This guy, the Colonel says, is a piece of shit.

—Colonel, Fritz says, I am asking you, please, please, don't start in.

—Got you fooled, huh? the Colonel says. Duped. I can see right through him. Beneath the attitude and the education and the sweet tenor voice is pure shit. And it makes me want to puke all over the room.

—My parts, my title, and my perfect soul shall manifest me rightly, Eddie says.

The Colonel reaches across the bar and grabs a bottle. He swings at Eddie's head, but Fritz steps in front of the Colonel, blocks the bottle, draws a heavy antique pistol from inside his shirt, and cracks the Colonel in the head. The Colonel crumples and falls spread-out on the floor.

Fritz shakes his head. —There used to be three Colonels. Some of you boys take the Colonel to his couch.

—Never seen a pistol like that, Eddie says.

—Chinese, Fritz says. Wanted one for years. Kept the eyes open, and got a hell of a price. I'm a collector.

Eddie gulps his beer. —I'd forgotten there was such a thing. The house, the beautiful objects beautifully displayed, the family. The happy family.

Fritz sits down, bends forward, his face next to Eddie's face. —Lemme tell you something.

—Yeah, Eddie says.

—You went wrong, man. All wrong. Now, how could anybody live like that? Christ, I just can't see it.

—Maybe I belong in a cage, Eddie says.

—I'm not talking about what you did. I mean, it's the betrayal. What did anybody ever do to you?

—I never meant to be wrong, Eddie says.

—You know they're out there. One, two, three. Same thing. Like fucking—like fucking scarecrows on a hill. They can't do nothing, but they're always in the background. You never get free of that.

—They're there, I'm here, Eddie says. That's all I got—all I got to go on.

Fritz snaps his fingers. His boy refills his glass. —This world is hard. You get that when you're young. If you got a brain, you know?

—Hard and harder, Eddie says.

Fritz's boy refills the beer pitcher.

—You did wrong, Fritz says, be clear on that. But at least you did something. Wanted some, got some. Have to hand it to you there.

—Er, Eddie says.

Fritz's face bulges like a hideous balloon. —They get you. Get you in a room and tell you what you did.

—Join up with me, Eddie says. We'll get others, too.

—What, have you been watching movies?

XVIII

Eddie wakes up. He is flat on his back on the bar, a drink in one hand and a dead cigarette in the other. His trousers are gone, and he is surrounded by burnt-out candles. Eddie sits up. Some of the candles fall.

The rec room is empty. He goes into the bathroom, pisses, looks in the mirror. There are blue lines on his forehead and cheeks. Eddie rubs his face: pool cue chalk.

He drinks some tap water, wanders around the empty rec room.

A hand sticks out from under one of the couches. Eddie stares: thick, hairy, veined, a gold band on a finger. He feels dizzy, squats, braces himself on the edge of the couch. Eddie grabs the hand, yanks.

Fritz glides across the floor. —Wha? He pulls out his pistol and points it at Eddie's face.

Eddie slaps the gun away. —Where are my fucking pants?

Fritz blinks. —Yeah. You checked out.

—My clothes?

—Dead to the world, so we gave you a wake. The boy put that BURY IN A.M. sign on you?

—My pants?

—Hell, they bury you in half a suit. Pants? Somebody put them someplace.

Eddie walks away. He looks behind the bar. Fritz snores. Eddie finds his soiled pants on the VCR. A hole has been burned through the fabric above the right knee.

The house is quiet. Eddie takes a soda from the refrigerator and goes out the back door. His watch is missing.

He sits on the stoop. The sun shines bright. Eddie finds a cigarette in his shirt pocket, lights it, opens the soda. He notices a birdhouse on a pole in the yard. Three stories and a roof shingled with tiny asphalt shingles. Multiple holes. Not one of those order-through-the-mail items. Hand-crafted, unique.

A wave of nausea. Eddie stands up, inhales deeply, tries to relax, inhales again. He stumbles to the plastic trash can beside the house, lifts the lid, vomits into the can. He vomits again. Eddie straightens up and immediately bends over the can again. The screen door slams.

—You're sick.

Eddie raises his head. It is Angela. —Fine, fine, Eddie says. He lowers his head and retches.

Angela goes inside.

Eddie clears his throat and spits. He wipes his mouth with the back of his hand.

Angela comes out and hands him a mug of tea and a paper napkin. —Maybe this will help.

Fritz comes out. —Heard you were a little under the weather. Anything I can do?

Eddie waves the empty mug. —Much better.

—Purged, eh? Best thing. Fritz yawns. That's what these parties are all about. All these guys sitting in their houses, they need to get out and blow off a little.

—I understand, Eddie says.

—Good for the head, Fritz says. For the brain. Veins, too. Massive dose of alcohol cleans out all the cholesterol and plaque. Not every day; that's too much. But once in a while, hell, you need it.

Eddie finds a surplus store in the strip mall and buys some multipocketed pants. Used, but durable. He changes in the dressing room, and stuffs his old pants in a trash can.

Eddie admires himself in the plate glass of a vacant storefront. Pants look fine, but the hair is a problem.

When the barber finishes clipping, Eddie's hair is cropped near the skull. The barber brushes Eddie's face, steps back to admire his work. —Nice and even, but something's missing. How about a shave?

—Ah, Eddie says.

—On the house.

The lather is warm and moist.

The barber pushes the chair up.

—Finished? Eddie says.

—Almost. He wraps a towel around Eddie's face. The bell over the door rings. Eddie jerks, tries to get up. The barber pushes him back into the chair.

The barber unwraps the towel. A slender young woman stands by the door.

—That's Sally, the barber says. She's buying me out.

Sally waves gently.

The splayed fingers shock Eddie. The hand remains in the air, floating free, although Eddie can clearly see that Sally's hand has returned to her side.

Eddie jumps up and presses a bill into the barber's hand. —Gotta bolt.

He starts up the hills that lead to Fritz's house. Eddie's breathing is labored. He sweats. His steps are jumpy.

At the top of the first hill, several long, low concrete buildings and a parking lot. Small islands in the center of the lot. The islands are encircled by curbing and covered with grass and trees. Eddie sits under a tree.

He leans against the rough bark, tilts his head back, tries to catch his breath. There is a gentle breeze. Eddie feels the sweat drying on his face. He looks up through the branches. The clouds part. Birds sing. Eddie feels the wind in the trees, the sway of high branches.

If he could, Eddie would stay here, breathing the fresh air. If he could talk to someone, make a deal, get his old job. They could set him up with materials, and he could stay here to capture the light and colors. Eddie can see a sort of purity. A purity he has often heard of in descriptions of places where the earth is pure and the sky is pure and the water is pure, in the pure land.

He gets up and walks, circles the base of the tree. Eddie steps off the curb. He is out of the trees.

Eddie can see the clear sky. He sees Deirdre. He realizes it is not Deirdre in the sky. It is Dolores.

Dolores superimposed on the dome of heaven, not a body or statue, but a stylized, two-dimensional Dolores of crumpled and resmoothed gold foil washed over with blue and white and sepia washes. The sky and sun shine through her. Eddie stands, unable to move.

—Wake up, Fritz says.

Eddie is waiting for something from Dolores. If she will speak. Sometimes it seems her lips are moving a little, but Eddie knows her lips are not moving and that she will not speak to him.

Fritz takes Eddie by the shoulders and shakes him violently. —Come on, let's go.

Eddie waits. For birds. Birds often bring signs.

Fritz has Eddie in a complicated hold. There is a nightstick across Eddie's throat. Fritz pulls. Eddie cannot resist. His eyes are forced downward. He gasps for air.

Fritz gets him in a car. —I don't mind telling you, you had me worried. Christ, what happened to your hair?

—Neat.

—I find you shorn, Fritz says, in those pants, staring at the fucking sky like a fucking turkey in a fucking rainstorm. What the fuck were you looking at up there?

—Long gone, Eddie says. Nothing there.

.   .   .

Eddie falls asleep in the guest room. He wakes when he hears the doorknob turn. A woman stands framed in the lighted doorway.

—Dolores, Eddie says. His eyes fill with tears.

—Are you all right? Angela says.

—Yes, Eddie says. I was dreaming.

Angela turns on the light. She has a tray. —I thought you might be hungry. I brought you soup.

—Thanks, Eddie says. Sorry for all the trouble.

Angela speaks softly. —Fly out of here. As soon as you're strong, get up and go.

—There's the boy, Fritz says. He is drinking coffee at the kitchen table. —Little lady had to go see her family. One of these so-called emergencies. Plenty of cereal or toast. Just have to bach it for a few days.

—I was thinking, Eddie says, I better head out.

—They'll dog your every step. That's no way to go.

—You have another way?

—I have a rec room.

—You got something for me, Fritz, lay it out.

Fritz laughs. —You're like a fish that asks where the fucking water is. He throws Eddie a folded newspaper. —Look through this. I have to make some calls.

Fritz walks out of the room.

—Don't tell me, Eddie says. If I could find the right pattern, then follow it. Do everything exactly right, because if there is one mistake, one little fuck-up, that is it. You have to start over. Try. Try and try. Begin. Start over. This time—

XIX

Eddie drums slowly on the table with the newspaper.

—Good for something, huh? Fritz says. Let's take a ride. We'll use your auld Olds.

Eddie starts for the driver's side.

Fritz blocks his path. —I know the way.

—Whatever. Eddie settles into the passenger seat.

Fritz tears out of the drive. —I might be able to put you on to something. What I ask is that when you have your look, you see it clear, with a fresh eye.

—I can do that.

—We've always gotten along, Fritz says. He follows a country road through the woods, swerves onto some ruts, takes the track as it winds down a hill, pulls up next to a black sedan in a dirt lot.

Eddie gets out of the car. A swift river flows near the lot. Tire ruts begin at the far end of the packed dirt and lead to a one-lane wooden bridge. Across the water, there is a clearing and a new, large log house. A screened porch runs around three sides of the house. A stone chimney is built into the remaining side. Little puffs of smoke rise from the chimney. There are utility buildings, a large wood pile, tilled garden, then the low shrubs, brush, woods. A new truck is parked in the driveway. A chow sleeps on the lawn. Deer browse in the forest. Birds sing.

A woman steps out onto the porch.

Dolores.

—You still with us? Fritz says.

Eddie looks. Fritz stands with a man in a dark suit.

—I know you, Eddie says. You're, uh, Businessman—

—Yes, the Businessman says.

—The Businessman of the—the—the—the—

—Whatever, the Businessman says.

—Only forty-five minutes from town, Fritz says. What you wanted? This is it?

—That woman, Eddie says.

—You two be friends, Fritz says, real good friends. After all, we're all human here.

—That's so true, Eddie says. He steps toward the bridge. —I can just, ah . . .

—One thing, Fritz says. Maybe we should dump the shit from the car. You know, clean slate and so forth.

—Absolutely, Eddie says. He steps back to the Olds, opens the trunk, begins taking things out. Fritz gets the stuff from the interior. They waddle, heavily laden, to the bridge and set their piles down. Eddie throws things into the water: fast-food containers, porno magazines, a broken shovel, rags, Bob's forty-five, Jim's nine-millimeter, Mr. Thompson's .357, a sawed-off twelve-gauge, a .308 carbine, a .410 derringer, a boot knife, a twenty-two revolver, a machete, a forty-four single-action, a cash box, an aluminum flashlight, a stun gun, a twenty-gauge double, a cash bag, a thirty-thirty, a click knife, a nine-millimeter short, a styrofoam cooler. Fritz whistles a soft tune. Everything sinks but the cooler. Eddie watches the white box run the swift course for a moment, then turns toward the house.

—One thing, Fritz says. He taps Eddie's chest.

Eddie laughs, takes the twenty-five from his shirt pocket, throws it as far as he can. —Maybe we should dump the car?

—Bad for the environment, Fritz says. Don't worry, I'll bury it for you.

Eddie starts slowly over the bridge.

—I'll walk you across, Fritz says.

He trails behind Eddie, singing sweetly:

> Many's the year I rambled alone,
> O'er plains and mountains, forsaken me home.
> Some think it sufficient to live for the lance,
> But I know a man alone's got no fucking chance.

Eddie steps onto the opposite shore.

They come in a blast. Men in the trees, on the roof, from the porch, the sheds, the woods, all firing guns. Eddie swerves, dodges, turns. He sees flashes. Fritz and the Businessman. Eddie spins in a wheel of fire.

The Businessman yells. —Hurry up, motherfuckers!

The Life

There had been no sun for three days, or five days. A week. A couple weeks. No sun or snow. Just dusk, dusk all the waking hours.

His wife tried to talk to him.

—It's this weather, he said. That, and the economy. And maybe the fucking sunspots.

—Aren't they weather? his wife said.

He had no reply.

She was after him to stop.

He would not stop.

He waited alone at the bus stop. All the passing cars had broken grilles. Some had cardboard where the grilles had been. Cars and dusk and slush.

An ambulance pulled up and stopped—parked—at the bus stop. Two big men got out. Their white pants were dirty, and they wore heavy boots and greasy dark nylon jackets. They looked like garage mechanics, and they grabbed him.

He tried to fight. They did not have a gun. They had him by the arms. He tried to kick, to get an arm free, to at least, for Christ's sake, throw a punch. They did not even have a knife. They got him in the ambulance and strapped him to a stretcher.

—I'll hunt you down like dogs, he said.

· · ·

He was strapped to a chair in a big room. There was a window. He saw walls, gray light, smokestacks, railroad cars, tracks, sidings, coal barges on the oily river—the whole dingy world.

His wife was there.

It was as though a blindfold had been removed.

—This is an intervention, his wife said.

Fortunately, he had no friends.

—We have no friends left, his wife said.

He hummed a little tune.

His wife went on at length.

He told himself, So this is how it is. He vowed to himself that he would not speak.

—You can not go on doing these things, his wife said.

—People get rich doing these things, he said.

—You won't, she said.

His legs were strapped to the chair legs, but he could rock the chair. He rocked back and forth, side to side. The chair fell. He pissed all over himself.

His boss came in. —There are some issues we have to deal with. I have to cut your job. Not entirely. I'll keep you on half-time, no benefits.

He opened his mouth.

—Tough break, the boss said, but you're lucky to just hang on. Wasn't your father with the company?

—Thirty-nine years, he said.

—Survived four changes in management, the boss said. Now how in the hell could he do that? Got to be a bit of a joke towards the end.

—You are destroying my life, he said.

—What can you do? the boss said. I remember the first time a guy hanged himself from the corporate sign. Quite

a shock. Some kind of symbol, I guess. Now we have a
half-time position just to cut 'em down and cart 'em off.

The boss raised his hands. —No reflection on you.

When he woke up, they were all there—his wife, the boss,
the ambulance men, a guy in company coveralls with a
slide projector.

The projector shone on a blank square of wall.

The slides: His desk blotter. Doodles. Blow-ups.
Sketches. Women. Naked women. Pictures from his
pocket diary, appointment book, notebooks. Women.
Men. Cartoonish, exaggerated depictions of sexual acts.

—You did this on my time? the boss said.

—Filth, his wife said.

—I was trying, he said.

The slides kept coming.

—This is what he makes, his wife said.

She covered her face with her hands and began to
weep. —I can't look anymore. I can't give any more.

—The company doesn't cover this. The boss put his
arm around her.

They walked to the door.

Everyone left.

He sat looking at the light on the wall and listening to
the projector. He had always known the future would
arrive and that it would be bad. But he had never expected it to be like this.

Franchise

The big signs were gone. But their steel skeletons rose over the lot. The building looked pretty good. Mostly brick and plastic. Windows covered with plywood. Across the street, a boarded-up car lot, abandoned factory, and burnt-out apartment complex.

Wayne walked to the back of the building. The lot was busted up; weeds grew through the cracked surface. The drive-thru speaker had been ripped from its plastic frame. Rotting wire dangled in the wind. At the edge of the lot, brush and a wooded slope. All this would be woods. Failed development.

Wayne followed a faint trail. Cans, bottles and rags littered the hillside. A mound of trash bags with a halo of flies. He could hear running water in the gorge. The banks were narrow ribbons of rock and sand. Broad stream, maybe thirty feet across. Wayne could not tell how deep it was. A log or part of a car frame stuck out of the water downstream. Wayne walked towards it.

He heard someone humming. Singing. Half-humming and half-singing. Something hit the water. Wayne stepped back into the brush. The singing stopped.

A slight man with wild gray hair and beard, torn baseball cap, stained work clothes. The man held a long cane pole. Fishing.

"Hey," Wayne called. "Getting any?"

The man half-turned.

Wayne noticed the fillet knife hanging from the man's belt. He stayed put.

"Why?" The man said.

"Just curious."

The man set the pole down, put one foot on it, and bent over a rock. He pulled up a piece of dirty clothesline, a crude stringer hung with fat carp. "Want to buy?"

"Don't think so," Wayne said.

"No money? I'll take it out in trade. What have you got for us to drink?"

"How'd you get so many?"

"Bait. It's all bait presentation."

The liquor store was small. Wayne looked for cut-rates, local gin and vodka, bourbon with Kentucky on the label and Wisconsin in the fine print. Three liters and he came out less than twenty-five bucks light.

Wayne left the bourbon and gin in the car and carried the vodka to the water. The man was still fishing. Wayne cracked the seal and handed the man the bottle. "What's your name?"

The man tapped the torn visor of his cap. "Bill, like on a hat." He pulled up the stringer. "Take your pick."

"That's okay," Wayne said. "We'll have a few drinks."

They were three-quarters through the bottle, and it was getting dark. A breeze came up off the water.

Wayne shivered. "Where do you stay?"

"I have places." Bill drank deeply. "That's where I come out ahead. I got my pick."

Laughing, they went up the trail. Bill said, "We need a go-round tank. Water goes round and round. Put your fish in there, water runs through them, cleans them. Gets all the mud and that out. Then you know what?"

Wayne laughed, slipped on some mud, grabbed a bush. "I know what."

"What?"

"I don't know."

"Then they ain't gray-looking. Gold. They look gold. And sweet. Man, you don't know how sweet that flesh is."

"It's the water," Wayne said.

Wayne looked at the plywood-covered window. "We need a hammer. Fucking sledge. Bust it to fucking hell and gone and we're inside."

"C'mon," Bill said. "You're drunk." He led Wayne to the back of the building and jumped up on a rusted-out dumpster. "Follow me." He hoisted himself onto the roof.

Wayne followed Bill up. He had to jump twice to catch hold of the roof.

Bill had a trap door open. "Careful, it's dark." He pulled a loop of rope out of the trap. "Catch the line and slide down. Wait till I'm down to start. Don't let go till you hit the bottom."

Wayne waited for the call, slid down the rope. Bill lit a candle. A couple more. He sat down on an inverted pickle bucket and motioned Wayne to another. They were in the kitchen. The grills and counters were gone. Capped pipe where the sanitary sinks had been.

Bill spread newspaper on the floor, took out his knife, cleaned the fish. Wayne drank, lit a cigarette.

He finished the bottle. "We got more booze in the car. Should have got some food, too. I'll go out when I've finished my smoke."

"Give me the keys; I'll go," Bill said.

Wayne did not want to climb back out. He handed over the keys. Bill went up the rope. The trap door banged open. Everything was quiet for a long time. Wayne wondered if Bill had taken the Comet.

Bill slid down the rope, the bottles jammed in his armpits. "Why didn't you tell me?"

"What?"

"Which you wanted."

"Who cares? The Chinese call it all wine." Wayne opened the gin.

Bill rooted around in the dark, lit a can of sterno, rigged a skillet over the flame with a homemade wire rack. "Bread, they say in England."

"What?"

"Call food bread there." Bill tossed a fish into the skillet. "Doesn't matter what kind."

Wayne handed him the bottle. "No, you're wrong. What you're thinking, you're thinking is, they call everything corn. That's what you're thinking of."

Bill handed Wayne the bottle.

"Any grain," Wayne said. "Like oats. They call oats corn. And the funny thing is they don't even have corn over there."

"That ain't true." Bill flipped the fish like flapjacks. "What you mean is meat."

"Fuck you," Wayne said. "Meat has nothing to do with it. Back then poor people didn't even eat meat."

"Back when?"

"When they called it corn. You know, when they started calling it corn in olden times."

"That's when they called it meat," Bill said. "Like, you know, the giant. The giant said, 'I'll drink his blood to make my meat.' "

"Giant?" Wayne said. "Goddamn. I never heard of any fucking giant."

Bill talked about the circular tank. Wayne concentrated on the fish and the bottle. He tossed the bones in the skillet and wiped his hands on his pants.

Bill looked at the bones in the pan, stopped chewing, looked at Wayne.

"I own this place," Wayne said.

"No shit."

"Really. My old man had it a long time. He's dead. Now it's mine."

"You can have the car dealer's across the way," Bill said. "Or the factory."

"I'm not taking anything away from you. I got it from him. It's really mine."

"Anything is possible."

Wayne shrugged. "Who knows."

"Maybe I could work for you," Bill said.

"Get this place going," Wayne said. "A restaurant."

"Food," Bill said, "on belts. Belt turns and the sandwich goes by. Man puts the catsup on. Again and again. All day long. Sometimes it seems like forever; that food never gives out."

"You'd be condiment king?" Wayne said.

"Better than that," Bill said.

"What can you do?" Wayne said.

Bill said, "I can find water with a stick."

. . .

They finished the whiskey and cigarettes. Bill wanted to take the skillet to the stream and scour it with sand. Wayne followed him out.

The sky was getting light. Wayne tripped on the broken asphalt and fell.

"Fuck," he said.

Bill helped him up. "Spring under here. Makes the ground shift."

"Sinkhole," Wayne said.

Bill dropped the skillet, went limp, bent at the knees, straightened up, stiffened stiff as a pointing bird-dog.

"What?" Wayne said.

Bill's eyes rolled back in his head. He breathed harder and harder. "It's about to happen," Bill said.

"Yes," said Wayne.

"But what," Wayne said, "is the meaning of it?"

Fishing Trips

Jim and Sam have planned the trip for months. The equipment shows this—the topographical maps mailed away for, the complicated first-aid kit, the nesting camper's cookware. All the equipment has been secured, wrapped in plastic, and taped or lashed in the twenty-one-foot aluminum canoe. The canoe has been painted bright red. Jim says this is to ensure visibility if the canoeists are lost. Sam holds the opinion that the bright color makes the canoe look as if it were made of fiberglass instead of aluminum. They didn't ask the man at the outfitter's where they rented the canoe two days ago. The issue becomes irrelevant now, when they are in the middle of a deep lake and the canoe strikes a submerged rock or log. The fishermen paddle quickly when this happens, and the bottom of the canoe tears open.

The fishermen are saved by their fisherman's vests, the multipocketed, khaki-colored flotation devices they bought at Kmart for this trip. They bob momentarily in the water, gasping and coughing, still shocked at how the canoe has sunk out from under them.

Jim calls, Are you okay?

Sam nods.

Both turn their heads and look along the shoreline.

Where should we head for? Jim says.

Sam tries to shrug, but he just bobs.

The fishermen swim for shore. Their vests keep them afloat, but the devices also seem awkward. The pine trees look distant, and it's hard for the fishermen to tell how much progress they're making.

Finally, the fishermen reach shore. There is a sandy area perhaps ten feet wide, and behind it weeds and grasses, and behind them the forest. Jim and Sam sit on the beach, panting. By Sam's watch it is 10:49 a.m. The air is warm and Jim estimates the temperature to be in the low seventies. Sam unzips his vest and pulls it off. He rolls it up, lies back, and uses it for a pillow. Jim imitates Sam. The fishermen lie there, looking at the sky. Jim takes a soaked and wrinkled cigarette package from his shirt pocket. He tears open the top and removes a broken cigarette.

Sam says, Is that the last one?

Jim tears off part of the cigarette and hands it to Sam. He lights each of their cigarettes with a lighter. The tobacco sputters and the paper bleeds brown, but the wet cigarettes stay lit.

When they've finished, Sam says, How far in do you think we are?

Hard to say, Jim says.

I think it'll be awhile before they look for us, Sam says. I mean weeks, Sam says. He stands up, then squats down on his heels. He empties his pockets. Sam has a red bandana, a small Swiss army knife, some keys, and a ballpoint pen. Jim has the same things, except instead of the ballpoint pen he has the cigarette package and lighter, and he finds a small plastic box of hooks in the Velcrosealed pocket of his fishing vest.

We'll make it. Sam looks around. He picks up the bandana and frays one edge of it with his knife. He tears it into thin strips. We'll knot these together for line.

They'll see the knots.

They won't know they're knots. Think of the Indians. They didn't have monofilament.

Okay, Jim says. I'll get poles. He walks into the forest. He is back in minutes with some gnarled sticks. Sam shakes his head. The best I could do, Jim says. The fishermen bait their hooks with aluminum foil from the cigarette package. After hours, the fishermen have two small fish. The fishermen take the fish with them when they go for firewood.

The camp seems permanent. The utensils, a few tin cans and two rough wooden trenchers, are near the fire ring. The lean-to looks solid. Two fishing poles are rigged in forked sticks, and Jim is trying to make a trotline of braided tree bark while Sam experiments with small deadfall traps. The fishermen have been keeping a calendar, but the fishermen didn't start until they realized they didn't know how long they had been there. The fishermen have not seen any other people, but they are confident that people canoe through this area all the time. The food is monotonous: fish, boiled acorns, dandelions, wild strawberries. The fishermen try to watch what the birds eat. The fishermen believe that any plant a bird can eat will not be poisonous to humans. The clear, blue water in the lake is good.

The fishermen have seen deer and a moose in the forest, and have found bear tracks near their camp. The bear tracks concern the fishermen. Jim wants to move up from the beach into the forest. Sam agrees that this might be wise, but he feels the fishermen should be near the fish and water of the lake. He suggests that the fires and human scent will keep the bears away. Jim says the fishermen should move on, perhaps circle the lake in hopes of finding some other people.

That, Sam says, is going against what they say. They say you should stay put and wait for help to come to you. He goes on to point out that the bear, or bears, have not come into the camp.

Jim goes into the forest and comes back with a birch sapling. He sharpens one end of the trunk and hardens the point in the fire. Sam watches him. Later, he makes a spear like Jim's.

The fishermen work together, using the wooden hoe and shovel they've fashioned to make a deer trap. The fishermen dig a trench and plant stakes with fire-hardened points in it.

Early the next morning, a deer falls into their trap. The deer is still alive. One of its forelegs is stuck through with a spike and there are two spikes in its abdomen. Its tongue hangs out and it shakes its head from side to side. Kill it, Sam says. Jim swings his spear at the animal. The blow hits the deer on the flank and lifts the deer off the spikes. The deer jerks its legs. It tries to stand. Sam swings his spear at the deer's head. Jim stabs the deer in the side and Sam smashes it on the neck. The fishermen keep doing this until the deer lies on its side, its wounded leg nearly severed, its coat covered with blood and dust. The fishermen stand there looking at the deer.

They bleed and skin the deer and decide to cook it whole in hopes that the meat will keep longer cooked.

The fishermen spit the deer on a green branch over a fire pit. Jim sets the heart and liver on hot rocks. He turns the organs after a few minutes. Sam tears the liver into two pieces and gives one to Jim. Jim tears the heart and hands a piece to Sam.

The carcass chars on the outside. Sam rips off a strip of meat. The inside is still raw. The fishermen break off pieces of the burnt layer and eat, making their way inward.

I I

After the first or second winter, Jim spots the tracks. It is morning, a little after dawn, and Jim is out to check some snares and the trotline. Sam is in camp, rubbing deer brains on a stretched hide. There are two sets of tracks. Both sets were made by the cleated synthetic soles of hiking boots.

Jim listens. He can't hear anything. He follows the tracks for a few yards, then stops again. Again he hears nothing. He follows the tracks like this for an hour or more, then backtracks to camp.

Sam and Jim follow the tracks until they hear voices. The fishermen dive into the brush. The fishermen wait for a while and then crawl until they reach the top of a small rise. The fishermen look down into the clearing where the man and woman have set up camp. The fishermen see an orange nylon tent and a backpacker's stove that burns bottled gas. They see a red fiberglass canoe next to the tent and a box of groceries hanging from a tree.

Sam motions toward the trail. He and Jim creep back slowly, then run to their own camp.

The fishermen come back that night. They wait to be sure no one is moving. The fishermen make their way down the rise, pick up the canoe, and run up the trail. No one comes after them.

III

By the end of the summer, the fishermen have two canoes, fishing rods, knives, and axes. They don't bother with food or clothing, although once Sam took a salt shaker.

Two fishermen are camped a few miles away. Sam and Jim have scouted the camp. The new fishermen leave early each morning and return at midday with their catch. It seems likely that the new fishermen have liquor, and it is always possible they will have guns.

Sam and Jim wait for a few hours after the sun has risen and go to the new fishermen's camp. They follow the trail and walk straight into the center of the camp. Jim cuts the box of groceries down from a tree and searches through it. Sam splits the side of the green tent with a fillet knife. He jumps back as the man inside jumps up. The tent is caught around the new fisherman's legs. He frees himself and runs past Sam to the woodpile. Sam runs after him. The new fisherman grabs a piece of birch from the pile and swings it at Sam. Sam stabs the fisherman in the stomach. Jim is behind the fisherman. Jim has a piece of wood. The fisherman stumbles forward and swings the stick again. It hits Sam in the face. Jim beats the man's head while Sam stabs.

I V

The chase goes on for days. Jim and Sam see a few of the men. The men wear camouflage clothing and carry guns. They have dogs. Jim and Sam burn what will burn in camp and throw the rest in the lake. The fishermen paddle the canoes out to the middle of the lake, sink one, and take the other to the opposite shore. They sink it in a few feet of water and go inland. The fishermen climb trees and keep watch.

At first, they are safe on the opposite shore. But then they hear dogs barking. Sam and Jim run. The fishermen run for hours, dodging through the woods. They look for water—streams, ponds, puddles—anything to throw off the scent. The dogs are behind the fishermen. After a while, they stop hearing the dogs. At night, the fishermen walk as quickly as they can down the open trails. Sometimes the fishermen crawl into thickets to sleep.

One morning, the fishermen see a lake, blue in the sun, below them as they stand on a wooded bluff. The fishermen are looking for a path to the water when the helicopter comes over them. The fishermen run along the bluff, see a steep path, scramble down. They hear dogs. At the base of the bluff there is a strip of woods and the narrow rocky beach. Sam and Jim dodge through the trees, looking back, looking up, looking for the helicopter. The fishermen cannot see or hear it. They hear only the hunters. The fishermen scramble over the rocks. They see the hunters. The hunters fire and keep firing. Jim grabs his abdomen and falls, bleeding. His body tumbles as it is hit. Sam jumps into the water and swims.

A History of Amnesia

At work, I work with chemicals that are dangerous. Known carcinogens. And that's just the tip of the iceberg. I asked the shop steward about it. But he was noncommittal. Hemmed and hawed, as somebody said.

I have the television set on. The sound is turned all the way down. Some men on the screen are fighting a fire. Could be chemicals going up. I am interested in their helmets, boots, and raincoats. Specialized gear. I wear specialized gear in my work as well. The state, as well as my employer, requires it. I certainly don't mind. According to union/management agreements, the company provides our gear, the locker rooms where we change, and the showers where we shower.

Of course, there is more to the place than that. The other workers, my fellow employees, and I aren't machines. We add personal touches. Many of my co-workers have taped posters or photographs on the insides of their lockers' doors. I myself have a mirror posted on mine for that neat appearance.

The main thing, the most noticeable thing of our "gear," is the white coveralls. These are, of course, required for all plant personnel. And there's more to them than appears to the casual inspector, as we employees were told during our orientation lectures. Most white coveralls are made of cloth, cotton, or the increasingly popular cotton and synthetic blends. But not ours. Ours are made of a woven cellulose-based polymer product that is five times as strong as ordinary cloth and impermeable to air.

My son's name is Josh. He lives with his mother, my former wife, in a house in a subdivision outside the city. That sticks in my mind because when I last saw him, he was doing division problems for homework. I remarked on this coincidence to my former wife. She was unimpressed. She was also unimpressed by the gift I had brought little Josh. It was a pair of white coveralls just like the ones I wear at work. "Get those out of here," she said. "You'll make all of us sick." I explained that these were new, even though it was obvious. Anyone could see they were still sealed in plastic.

My former wife had her television on when I was over there last. She had the sound turned up. A man was talking to some other man. I said, turn that down. She said, "No, it's part of Josh's heritage." Where does Josh's heritage end and everything else begin? I told my former wife that.

At work, in addition to the coveralls, and the tight-fitting somewhat embarrassing skull caps, we wear masks, gloves, and booties. The booties are made of the same material as the coveralls. Protective clothing, of course, reduces the risk of accidents. Skill is another factor. One must be very careful when dipping the plates. If the plates slip down the holding rod, or if the chemicals splash out of the vats, an accident could easily result. I try to appear to be as skillful as possible. This approach seems to serve me well. Sometimes I use it when I ask my former wife to engage in sexual intercourse with me.

．　．　．

I know I need help. Bill tells me the tree school now stands abandoned where it once flourished. It's not that far from town. But to get to it, one must know the turns and roads and tracks, the combination of routes that make the route. Once, Bill says, people came from all over the country to attend the tree school. They went around town asking questions. The natives knew better than to answer. The instructors were in town disguised as natives. They would answer questions only when they had selected a person as a candidate. The people didn't realize they were being watched, tested. Most of them were not selected. They did not understand the nature of the tree school.

I ask Bill was it featured on television. Perhaps on one of the news shows or maybe even a documentary. Bill waves his hand. No, no, he says. Not this tree school. Maybe some of the others got press. Some of the imitations, perhaps. But this tree school, Bill assures me, is the genuine article.

This school had its predecessors, Bill says, but not in this country. This tree school is the heir to the classical tree schools of Europe. Or it was, before it closed down. Now the site remains, but the instructors are gone, lost, scattered, or dead.

But, I say to Bill, what about the site? We could go there, couldn't we?

Bill shakes his head. There isn't much to it. I'm afraid you'd only be disappointed.

I picture it at work while I'm supposed to be watching the gauges or dumping the sludge. I picture the tree school as it was — a group of dedicated men and women isolated in the wilderness to pursue their vision.

This tree school, I say to Bill, how big is it? What's the scale? Bill is hesitant. I push him. It's very important to me, I say. He mumbles and walks off.

There's nothing there any more, Bill says. It's all been over for a long time.

Bill, I say, just take me out there once. I only want to make a sketch.

A sketch, Bill says. What for?

I'm making a model, I say.

I buy a sketchbook and pencils and hunting socks and sturdy walking shoes and a surplus musette bag. But this is the tip of the iceberg. What about the mental and psychological preparation? The hours of research at the local community college that prove fruitless? The meditation? Contemplation?

Bill picks me up at dusk. He drives the old Dodge truck, one hand on the wheel, the other on a pint of whiskey. I have a pint of my own. We follow the pavement until it ends, turn on to a dirt road in the woods that becomes ruts and then nothing.

We walk, Bill says.

He gets out.

Lock her up, he says.

He plunges through the woods as though he's on a path. Brambles scratch me; it feels like there's a cobweb stuck to my face. Bill whispers, quiet. I stop for a second to catch my breath. He doesn't seem to make any noise.

It seems like hours. I expect a clearing. There is no clearing per se. A small clearing is all. Maybe the size of a table top. Maybe a little bigger.

Here it is, Bill says.

I look around.

Nothing to see, he says. Told you so, he says.

I look up into the trees and see them. Bill takes a step back. A small wooden platform, gray in the moonlight, high up on a birch. But there's more to it. A pulley.

Let's, I say.

What? Bill says.

We're here, I say.

Bill unbuttons his shirt. The black rope is coiled around his waist. He twirls as he plays it out with his hands. He puts one end in his teeth and shinnies up the birch.

Tie a loop in that end for your foot, he says as he threads his end through the pulley.

He hoists me to the platform and signals me to be quiet. He gestures with his hands, encouraging me, I take it, to look around. I look down. Bill puts his hand under my chin and pushes my head up. He moves his other hand from side to side. I look. At first I see trees. Branches and leaves. Then I notice another platform. And another. I look up. Some platforms are set higher than the ones I'm on. There are lower platforms as well. I realize that there's a network, a complicated set of interrelations. Bill reels in some clear, nearly invisible line. I look at the stars through the foliage. Bill has some sort of black nylon harness. He begins to buckle me in.

Really something, he says, infinitely more complicated than you'd expected.

He tightens the straps around my shoulders.

No, he says, don't talk. I know what you're feeling.

He cinches the belt around my waist. Ready?

I'm screaming. Flying. I break through branches.

Bill is on the platform above me, talking.

Bill says, Certain theories put forward our ancestors as nocturnal tree-dwelling creatures. Feeling better? Takes a minute, I know, to get your bearings. A certain equilibrium to overcome.

He does something with a ratchet. I start to swing in a wide circle.

Likewise, Bill says, some cultures have used the tree as a metaphor for the universe. Now I'm not here to attack either of these positions. But our greater sophistication allows us to see the various components as working together, and, in effect, perhaps the metaphor of a constellation is more suitable for the tree school than vice versa.

I'm spinning faster and faster in wider arcs. Branches fly at me. I block with arms, legs.

But that's not the point, Bill says.

I'm bouncing off one trunk into the next. I see stars. I can't breathe. I try to get the breath to beg.

A certain tension, Bill says, between the strict applicability of these techniques and your situation.

I was having a little trouble with my knees, and Karen said we should go see the mountain-lion lady. At the time I was sitting in one of those chrome and canvas chairs in her living room. It was a sort of a camp chair in the style that's in style now—or was, anyway. Plus, I was half-ignoring her, for reasons I'll get to later. So I wasn't really listening to Karen. I was looking through a magazine, one of several that she got in bundles from the coast.

You'll like it, she said. It's at the state park in the natural amphitheater. Are you ready? Kar said.

. . .

It was a fair distance to the state park. But the traffic wasn't too bad. I parked in a paved lot. Before I got out of the car, I slipped my revolver into the old musette bag Kar used as a purse. Not that I was worried, but I like to be careful in the woods.

There was a redwood sign with yellow letters that said:

NATURAL AMPHITHEATER →

The arrow pointed to a trail. It wasn't paved, but it was covered with something.

What's this stuff? I said.

Wood chips, Kar said.

Why is that? I said.

Instead of answering, she punched me in the shoulder. We followed the path up a hill, then down the same hill. Nobody else was on the trail. Kar admired the vegetation. I told myself rhymes, some cadence, because my knees were bothering me. It came to me to say something to break the monotony.

The amphitheater's all natural? I said.

Huh, Kar said.

I said, I say this amphitheater is natural. One of those deals that was created by a glacier, or by wind blowing sand at a mountain for countless generations.

We climbed the log steps until we found places on a log bench. The people in the crowd were equipped with radios, thermos bottles, and those coolers that are so popular today.

Is there a picnic component? I said.

No, Kar said. Anyway, not that I know of. There wasn't anything in the paper about it.

Well, I said, it's kind of suspicious, isn't it?

I scanned the crowd for vendors. I noticed some media crews along the edges of the amphitheater. They were slung down with cameras, zipped up in their multipocketed canvas vests which recalled specialized commando gear. Men in blue coveralls were setting up speakers, low tables, a slide projector and screen. A woman in khaki approached the microphone. She was wearing high boots, jodhpurs, and a bush jacket. Everyone clapped. They stood up. Kar was standing clapping.

I stood up too. Who is she? I kept saying. Kar was clapping and whistling.

The applause died out and we sat down. I asked again.

The mountain-lion lady, Kar said.

The mountain-lion lady began her slide presentation. Most of the slides were pictures of mountains or mountain lions or both. She had given the lions names. She talked about the animals' individual personalities and the threats that faced the species.

Who is to blame? the mountain-lion lady said. You are to blame, she said. She swung her hand at us. The audience applauded wildly. My knees ached. I was afraid they would stand up again. A man in coveralls brought out a box on wheels.

Now, the mountain-lion lady said, to continue my work, I have to leave the mountains and do these disgusting fund-raisers. Here's what you want, she said patting the box. It's here, caged and prostituted, for your appetites. Let's get this spectacle over with. I can not stand your human stink.

She pulled up one end of the box. A mountain lion jumped out. A murmur went through the crowd. The mountain lion snarled. A man in coveralls handed the mountain-lion lady a pink hula hoop. The mountain-lion lady shouted something. I couldn't understand the words. The mountain lion leaped into the stands. People started trampling each other. The mountain-lion lady laughed. I reached for the revolver. I heard shots and shoved Kar down. I stood and took aim. It was hard with the people, the panic. The mountain lion was slashing her way up the stands toward me. I fired. I heard more shots from somewhere. The revolver got away from me. The animal was almost at me. I lunged for the gun, but could not get my hands on it. The other gunman appeared to be standing on a grassy knoll. I screamed to the media crews, for God's sake, get a picture!

I took to the back steps. Don't misunderstand me. These were indoor steps, a staircase, if you will, carpeted with thick, musty, wine-colored carpet of indeterminate origin. A bit, perhaps, of the false orientalism of the type popular in department stores some thirty years ago or more. I would not speculate on price.

So there I sat, tall boy in hand, staring out the combination storm/screen door at the low weed- and brush-covered hill behind the building. The cool evening air drifted in, and the setting sun cast a glow over the brightly colored trash that stood out against the dead brown of the weeds. A part of a hula hoop or garden hose shone bright green, and the plastic transmission fluid bottles were turquoise in the dusk.

. . .

He was leaning against the cinderblock wall, his back to me, speaking into the pay phone. I noticed his coat. It was like a camouflaged coat.

I started quietly toward him, not wanting to disrupt his conversation. He turned quickly. One hand went into his jacket. He hung up the phone. A little business call.

Hey, okay. I stepped back.

No, really. I couldn't help but notice your approach. His hand was still inside the jacket. He was wearing a brown hat tilted over his eye. One side of his face was dark, shadowed.

Nice coat. Get it out at the mall?

No, imported.

Has that look. A sort of continental flair, eh?

He walked toward me.

So what is it?

You were the guy, I said.

That's enough, he said. Certain acts of recognition should be left to the experts.

Acts? I said.

Patterns, he said.

He was standing directly in front of me. His face wasn't shaded, as I had thought. Two rows of tattoos ran from his forehead to his chin. They crossed to form an X, meeting at his eye. I noticed these inch-wide bands were chains of smaller Xs. He looked at me looking at them.

Go ahead. Ask, he said.

I'll be the first to admit I could be mistaken. But, perhaps Kiowa, I said.

He laughed.

All right, I'm out on a limb here, original Polynesian work. Tahiti, maybe, or the Marquesas. Maori.

There's a question of precision on a job like this. You

got to look at the match-up, huh? Near infinite precision. Well, maybe you're thinking at one time that was impossible. You're thinking about the craftsmanship angle on that one. Looks good, but don't look too close. Closer you get, the worse it looks. Some bad spacing. Uneven gaps. He shook his head. People like you kill me. You're wrong, understandably wrong, but wrong all the same. You're living in the Stone Age. I'm talking about micro-spaced, fully equalized, computer-generated models. Models maybe, or is it full actualization? You tell me. Look as close as you like, he said.

It all seems so jumbled up. It started with Karen. After she saw the mountain lion killed, she became sullen — tense, depressed, withdrawn. I'd call and ask her out, but she'd say she just didn't feel like doing anything. Initially, I thought nothing of this, but in time the pattern became evident. I resolved to do something, busy though I was with my own pursuits. Fortunately, my fears were allayed.

Kar called one evening and invited me over. I need you, she said.

Oh, surely there's no rush, I said.

Right now, she said.

The apartment looked the same. The card table and folding chairs, the vinyl-covered hassock from Woolworth's. In one corner there was a picture leaning on one of those kids' green blackboards with the alphabet along the top and bottom. The Aa and Mm stuck out on top. It was Nn and Zz on the bottom.

He got in. I started the car. But it stalled. I'd been having a lot of trouble with it. I wasn't sure what to do. Know anything about cars? I said.

He said, Not really. I work near water mostly. Boats are more my line.

I nodded. It was dark. The car was making a kind of grinding sound.

X shook his head. Shot, he said. I didn't want to tell you back there. I popped the hood. I didn't have the heart for it. It's all shot—oil pump, rings, pistons, tranny. What you got—you got a wreck. Sorry, can't stand here. Got to bolt. Listen, though, you need some reliable transport.

I found myself with more free time. There was work. The storage facility was as busy as ever, and the future promised more work, more materials to be stored. I took to going out for the odd beer with my supervisor, Bill. We'd stop after work at a small tavern and share a pitcher or two. Bill told me not to worry.

I thought. I thought about X. I thought about my car. This, of course, was all an evasion. What really worried me was X. I wanted to talk to him some more. He made an impression, face it. But mostly Kar. That was the main thing.

Get a new car yet?

X had stepped up behind me in line at the convenience store. I didn't even know he was there.

It'll be a while. A matter of time. I've been riding with Bill for now.

You don't need to explain. I may be able to help if you want a lift out of this hole.

X drew me aside. We were outside by now, of course, but still he drew me aside, into the shadow of the corner of the building, as it were. On the opposite side of the building from the pay phone.

I'm negotiating, okay? That's all I want to say, all I can say, at the moment.

I don't want to pry, I said.

No problem. Just let it go. Projects in the works, okay?

We walked toward the deserted downtown area. I looked at every car we passed, sizing them up. There was price to consider, no denying that, but safety features and luxury were not to be overlooked either. I guess I wanted something that suited me, overall.

He said, I see you have questions, questions, questions. But you know what? You're not sincere. Don't ask me unless you're sincere.

Perhaps he was right. I decided I'd make it up to Kar. I crept up the carpeted stairs of her building. No one heard me. I leaned into the door bell. Kar opened the door wide, and I shot her picture with my Instamatic. The flash blinded her; she blinked.

What's wrong with you?

I wanted to make up, I said.

So you scare the shit out of me.

I took your picture, I said.

No kidding, she said.

Maybe it was true. I pondered it. Sincerity. I looked it up in the dictionary. I went to the library. I bought a friend-ship card, and stapled the picture of Kar in the doorway to it. I signed it sincerely and mailed it. But she didn't call. She'd had enough. The damage was done.

Bill took a job at a new facility out West. I bought a used VCR from a guy who was selling them off a truck in the parking lot of the mini-mart and took to staying home nights. At first I rented comedies. But they didn't cheer me up. I seemed to have trouble following them, like I wasn't in on the jokes. I started to get dramas, then foreign movies, anything. It was the noise I was after. Needless to say, my drinking increased.

Then one night I saw a glimmer of hope. A revelation, as it were. One dubbed foreign guy was screaming at another. He said the guy should prove his sincerity. The guy agreed, pulled out a knife.

X opened the door to my apartment.

Hey, I need some help, he said.

His truck was an old pickup with an oversized wooden structure built over the bed. The wood was gray and warped. The whole thing seemed to be leaning to one side.

This is it.

We got in and he drove to the storage facility. He backed up to a loading dock in a restricted area. The door was already open. We loaded the truck with crates labeled Danger.

He handed me a sawed-off double from under the seat and touched the wires to start the engine.

We began to speak other languages.

Seasonal

He caught my hands, both of them, in one hand, Mike says.

—Uh huh, Henry says.

—I tried to kick him, but he got my leg with the other hand. Caught me right under the knee.

—Yeah.

—So I'm on one foot. Hopping. He's got his hands full. He leans forward and smashes his head into my face.

—Head butt. Okay.

—I go back. He lets go my hands, grabs my face, gouges my eye.

—I know that one. Thumb'll grind ya and blind ya.

—I go down. He's kicking me in the stomach, the ribs.

—You thought you were tough, Henry says.

—I was drunk.

—You thought you were tough, but you were just drunk. Henry laughs.

Henry was semi-pro once. Some people say he did some time. When he was younger. Meaner. Now he's calm. Laughs a lot. Very active in his church.

Mike doesn't stop at O'Halloran's. He glances out the window of the Dart as he goes by. Too crowded. He heads straight for Gina's house.

—What happened?

Mike shrugs.

She touches his jaw. Bruises. —They're all swollen.

—Shit, you should see my ribs.

—You idiot.

—Well.

—This is stupid, Mike.

He has a set of books. Almost a set. Fourteen of the twenty volumes. *Complete Guide To Home Repair, Maintenance, and Construction.* Volume a month at $17.95 each. He studies some, glances at others. Mostly he looks at number six, *Masonry and Foundations.*

—You look bad, Henry says.

—Yeah.

—Gonna be sick? Henry pushes a styrofoam cup across the table.

—No. Mike pushes it back at Henry. He looks at the tinfoil ashtray.

—Fight?

—I stayed home.

Henry laughs. —Stay in and drink. That's step one.

—Forward or back?

—You know which.

They take two shovels out. That's all. Dig trenches for irrigation pipe. All fucking day. Mike stops for a minute at O'Halloran's on the way home.

He's late getting to Gina's. As he comes up the front steps, the porch light goes off.

—I don't know, you know, she might feel different about this after a while.

—You got a decision to make.

—Well, I wanted to ask you, Henry.

—Find the truth.

—They say you—

—Doesn't matter. I found the truth. That's it.

—It's not that simple, though.

—You're in a man's house, he makes the rules. You go by the rules. It's his house.

Restore a car. Something nice. Take it piece by piece. Be proud of it. Totally rebuilt, custom interior, leather tuck-and-roll upholstery, metal-flake paint.

But so impractical. No money. Or real tools. Or place to work. Or knowledge of where to begin.

Mike shoveling. Henry squats on the ground, sorting pipe. Mike hits a rock.

—You know where you're going? Henry says.

Mike pries it loose.

—Keep on, somebody'll kill you. Get a gun on you. Or a knife. Or you crash your car.

—I don't drink and drive.

—Never? Just once, all it takes.

—Okay, Mike says.

—You should look for another way.

—Okay, okay, okay, okay.

—Listen, Henry says, you don't want to talk, you don't bring it up.

Mike squares off a piece of paper with a Magic Marker and maps out a schedule. Home at 5:35, shower, supper, exercise, TV, bed. He tapes the schedule to the refrigerator and goes to the grocery store.

.   .   .

It works for a couple of weeks.

They talk about TV.

—What I don't get, Mike says, is why Liberace was so popular. I thought just old ladies watched him.

—Uh uh, everybody watched his show.

—Why, though?

—It was the fifties. People wanted to see something that was different.

—You watch him?

—Seen him.

They sit quietly for a minute.

—Said in the TV book everybody thought he was all right, a nice guy.

Henry nods. —Nice man, nice man.

The rock won't give. Mike swings the shovel like a baseball bat and hits the rock with the blade. The recoil hurts his hands. He hits the rock again and again and the shovel's handle snaps.

Henry shakes his head.

They go to the hardware store the boss uses. Henry chooses a shovel. Mike looks around. He wants to price a folding knife.

Mike works every night. And Saturdays. Some Sundays. He wants to quit. If he goes out, he thinks he should be home trying to finish. After a while he stops going out.

He gets some stuff—a resinous epoxy-like product that's supposed to be the future of auto body repair.

.   .   .

It's cold. November. The season will end soon for Mike. Henry works year-round, plowing snow in the winter. Mike's not sure what he'll do. Something inside. Warm. Maybe a warehouse job. No factory work.

Every Christmas Henry's church sells wreaths.

—You order now, later we deliver.

—But they're fresh, right? I mean, that's why there's the time lag?

—You think I'd sell you an old wreath? Yeah, they're fresh. Besides, they got that frost stuff sprayed on them. Last a year if you want.

—Okay, put me down for one.

—No pressure.

—Put me down.

He gets a book called *Great Art of Western Civilization* from the library. Looks through it. Takes his time.

Last day of the season he still hasn't found anything.

Henry shakes his hand. —Been good to work with you.

—You too, man.

—One minute. Henry goes to his car and pops the trunk. He takes out a wreath. —Here's yours.

It's big, maybe three feet in diameter, frosted pine boughs with a red velvet bow.

—You be tame, Henry says. Stay calm. You'll get it.

—Yeah, Mike says.

—Well, thanks Henry, he says.

President

No comparison is apt, the president says.

The president keeps a treasure, a crystal automobile, at his secure retreat in the woods. The automobile is a full-sized, four-door sedan with automatic transmission, V-8 engine, four-barrel carburetor. Everything but the tires is translucent crystal. The car's secret inner operations are visible to the naked eye. As the vehicle moves, the crystal picks up frequencies. Hums.

Only the president drives this car.

The pleasure diminishes in time. Flames and fumes sully the engine compartment and exhaust system. The crystal fouls, stained black, gray, dirty brown, and yellow. The president drives less and less.

The president drives fast. There is no moon, and he has ordered the concealed security lights shut off. He takes the turn too quickly. The car flies, hits the brush, smashes into the elm. The president knows what is happening. That it must happen. That he will survive intact.

—Destiny, the president says as they strap him to the stretcher. —No man can resist.

The president's brain is monitored. He sleeps deeply for forty-eight hours, wakes refreshed, dons his dressing gown, takes coffee at the horseshoe-shaped table with his advisors. The advisors inquire, gently but manfully, about the state of his health.

—Action, the president says, purifies the blood.

He steps out, his inner circle trailing behind him.

—Car! the president shouts.

A security man whispers in his ear.

The president nods, strides majestically, gown flapping, to the maintenance area. He finds the car covered, pulls the tarp away. The crystal engine block is shattered. Oil and transmission fluid drip from the scarred body. The president pulls a small chip from the smashed bumper and slips it into the pocket of his robe.

—Leave her to the elements, he says.

The president follows the necessary observances.

The president recalls his modest beginnings.

The president has nightmares about motor oil.

Things go badly.

—Plant a potted palm, the president says.

He goes by helicopter, airplane, limousine, train, car, bus, bicycle. The president and his wife are long estranged. He lives in a blockhouse decorated with photographs of spark plugs. Something comes around at night for loose food.

—Scavengers, the president says. They come in darkness to undercut my policy.

Stick

A priest, for example. Priests' collars, the Roman ones, are treated with a plastic substance. This priest had a problem with the collar, with the rubbing. A rash. Easy to imagine how it gets worse. The priest cannot complain about it. He has to wear the collar. So the priest orders more collars. Goes through a variety of styles, heights, trying to ease his condition. All for naught. The priest falls at the altar, and when the collar is loosened to give him more air, there it is. Cancer.

He dresses in his commando sweater and commando pants and commando boots, and straps on his commando watch and gathers his rod and tackle for a trip to a suburban lake. He checks the oil and coolant and tires and heads out.

He gets a few bluegills and leaves a sucker in the county garbage can. Stops for chili and beer at the lakeside tavern. Sees a black shoe in the road. Car with an I Love My Family bumper sticker. He cleans the fish in the kitchen sink, wraps them, puts them in the freezer to freeze.

His wife comes home late from work. —I love your get-up, she says.
     —I brought home fish for the pot.
     She gets a beer from the fridge, sinks into a chair.

—And your day? he says.

—That car you bought died on me twice.

He does not say anything.

—Big mistake, she says. Piece of shit.

He shifts his chair so he can stare at the knobs on the stove. She is right. He knows that she is right.

He wakes in the middle of the night. She snores. The clock clicks softly. His leg hurts. Pain radiates downward from the knee and upward from the ankle. He changes positions. But there is no relief. He touches the knee, the shin, the ankle.

He hikes to the grocery store, gets herbal tea, crackers, mineral water, soda, lemonade powder, cigarettes, a lean steak. He hopes to walk off the pain. But the leg does not feel any better. Foot drags. He fumbles through the security doors of his building, ascends the anciently carpeted stairs with difficulty, his empty hand on the railing, pulling his weight up a step at a time. Free of the staircase, he thinks he can make the short stretch of hall to his flat.

He falls.

Cans and bottles roll on the floor. This has never happened before. He struggles to his knees. But the leg gives out. He falls, all the way down. He coughs hard. During the fit, he sees red lightning bolts. He catches his breath and falls asleep.

Someone's hand is in his pocket. His pants. He flops about trying to resist.

—Quiet, now, a woman says.

—Yes, a man says. Here are the keys.

It is the neighbors, Mr. and Mrs. Fassbinder.

—You rest, Mrs. Fassbinder says.

—We are here to help, Mr. Fassbinder says.

They drag him into the apartment and wrestle him onto the couch.

—Should we call an ambulance? Mrs. Fassbinder says.

—No, he says, no doctors.

Mr. Fassbinder nods. —I understand.

Mrs. Fassbinder gets a pillow from the bedroom, lifts his head, jams the pillow beneath it.

—I notice, she says, the many beautiful photographs on your bureau.

—May I? Mr. Fassbinder says.

The shinbone is bent. He can feel it twisted inside his flesh. He sits up, pushes himself into a standing position. The leg twists away from him; his foot points backwards. He takes a step, falls, crawls on all fours, twisted leg trailing him to the kitchen. She must hear him, the groans and whines and shrieks, but the bedroom door stays shut.

He hacks down the broom with a meat cleaver. He practices with it, close to the counters, walking the length of the kitchen and back.

He goes to the bedroom. The leg is so twisted the foot is upside down. The lace of his shoe catches on the carpet. He leans in the frame and taps the door with his switch.

No answer.

He pushes the door open.

She sits in a rocking chair. The television is going.

He waves the stick. —I made a prosthesis, he says.

—You allowed them in, she says. They violated the privacy of our home.

—I could not stop them, he says.

—Not everything is a joke, she says.

—I do my best, he says.

She wipes her face with the back of her hand. —You had your chance, she says.

The leg is curling up like ash.

He takes a step to her. One step.

The leg falls off.

The boiler engineer's arms are covered with tattoos and thick, black hair. That dull, constant pain. Nothing at first, perhaps a pulled muscle. He lifts weights. As time passes, the muscle might be torn. Then the engineer knows it is not a muscle, but his ulcers. The kids are at that age, and he worries. Like any parent would. Finally he goes in, and they open him up. Spread all through him — liver, spleen, pancreas, kidneys.

All shot.

Fat Boy

Every cent was gone and he was down to the food in the cupboard. He had three weeks left on the rent, ate tuna fish and rice for breakfast, brushed his teeth with salt, rolled a cigarette. The heart went out of him.

He caught his neighbor in the front hall by the mailboxes and borrowed bus fare from her.

The bus ride was like all bus rides.

A glass and steel box that predated prettifying archways and cornices. He knew this public austerity well, and the woman at the desk. He had had words with her once, but she had forgotten him.

He filled out the forms and took a chair. These chairs were new: plastic shells covered with coarse black cloth. Hair, bits of paper, dirt caught in the fiber. He brushed the chair off carefully, hoping to dislodge any vermin that clung to the fabric.

There were posters of soldiers. He admired their muscles, guns, berets, but he was too old now. Not that he was that old. Anyway, it happened to everyone. All in good time. Perfectly natural.

The crowd was thicker and more diversified than when he had last visited — every level of the social strata. He paged through a telephone book to pass the time.

The call came and he almost leapt from the chair. He

had it—forward motion. The worst was over; now it would be step by step.

He walked through the doorway, the arch, into a dull maze of cubicles.

"Mr. Bigpower," he called, "it's me. I'm back."

Heads stuck out of cubicles.

"Where is he?" he called. "Where have you hidden the Powermaster?"

A man came out from behind a partition. "Be quiet, or you will be removed."

"I am looking for Mr. Bigpower."

The man shook his head. "He is long gone," the man said and motioned toward two men in the doorways of cubicles. "We run things now."

The men were slender and pale with receding hair and clear-plastic-framed glasses. They wore white shirts and pastel ties and tan trousers and brown shoes.

He looked from one man to another and back again. He stepped back, turned, and looked at the other workers. A bland lot.

The man who spoke ushered him into a cubicle. The man sat at the desk; he sat in the client's chair. The man fiddled with the computer keyboard and said, "I am the director of services." He tapped the plastic nameplate on his desk. "You may call me by my name or title; I have no preference."

"Well, Director—"

The man looked up and snapped, "Mister Director!"

"Mr. Director, I—"

"Enough," Mr. Director said. "I have your file on-line. You did know Bigpower. Been around for years, I see. Sadly, you are not one of our success stories."

"I did my best."

"I'm certain of that. As you know, there is a recession, and your skills are, frankly, in large measure, antiquated. But do not despair—we can have you out on the box load tomorrow morning."

He knew the box load, the hundred-pound lifts. "I junked my car and, you know, the buses don't go out that way. Too far."

"They have a shuttle now."

"I have loaded. My back is shot."

"The complainer with his whine."

A new voice. "Trouble here?"

He looked to the door. The Two Others pushed into the cubicle.

"Just the tired old routine," Mr. Director said.

The First Other shook his head.

"What can you expect?" The Second Other said. "He goes all the way back to Bigpower."

"Pathetically predictable," Mr. Director said. "It is as if they stamp these people out somewhere."

"What brand do you drink?" The First Other said.

"He flinched," The Second Other said. "We got him."

"Got the brand, got the man," Mr. Director said. "Most don't drink today, or smoke. He doesn't care about taking responsibility for his own health."

"Okay," he said, "put me on the box load tomorrow. I'll do my best."

Two days later he was back, his hand coated in bandage.

"Again?" Mr. Director said. "You are wasting my valuable time."

"I tried," he said. His voice warbled.

"There are people out there," Mr. Director said, "who really need work."

"I did my best," he said, "but I hurt myself." He began to weep.

"Look at this," Mr. Director called to The Others. "We have a crier."

The Others crowded into the cubicle, laughing.

"When Bigpower was here," he said, "you got a job or you didn't. He'd hardly look at you, much less talk. And he'd never put a man my age on the box load."

"His age?" The First Other laughed.

"You are a failure," The Second Other said. "It's written all over you."

"All over him?" Mr. Director said. "That's nothing. Hell, it's built into him."

"What do you go?" The Second Other said. "Two-ten? Two-thirty?"

He bit his lip. "One-ninety. But I'm going to drop off. Get back into shape."

"Hey, Fat Boy," Mr. Director said.

Mr. Director and The Others laughed.

They told him there might be something. Even for the one-armed Fat Boy. He waited in his plastic lawn chair by the free-with-a-magazine-subscription telephone. Some time went by with him beside that plastic telephone. Then Mr. Director called and asked if he was ready to work. He said his hand was nearly healed.

"That might work against you," Mr. Director said. "I'm pitching you as crippled but willing."

"I won't give you away," he said.

The bus was late. He left with time to spare, but the bus was late, and then its engine started smoking, and everyone had to get off and wait for another bus to come out and save them.

"Hey, Fat Boy," The Supervisor said, "you're late."

He tried to explain.

"Don't tell us your inner life," The Supervisor said. "Here." He pointed to a pallet jack. "Pull this with the good hand. Figure out how to steer it. Every day, you pull this where we tell you. Make the motion. All the rest, you'll never know."

He did as he was told. Every day. With the good hand. He learned to accept the cyclical routine. The other workers got to know him.

Over the years he saw them come and go. The new ones came in, and the old timers always introduced him.

"Say hello to Fat Boy," they said.

He pulled the pallet jack and smiled and wiggled his withered free arm.

Trains of the Future

After hours Friday, everybody long gone, he was cleaning out his cubicle.

The company provided him with boxes, strong fiberboard boxes with handle holes and full square lids, the kind used to store files. Those boxes, he had seen them at the office supply store, went for three, four bucks apiece.

They took everything, without mercy, but they gave him the boxes.

He filled two with his stuff and labeled and sealed three empty ones. They might come in handy.

Victor stood in the doorway of the cubicle. —Clear it out. I'm locking down.

Victor had worked at the prison outside town before he got on with this company.

He was sick. Sick of the house, sick of the days, sick of the time, sick of himself. Sick. He burned 7.9, the current official unemployment rate, into the back of his hand with a cigarette.

One could not go on like this. One could not isolate oneself, lock oneself out, box oneself in. Life was passing him by; he was too far outside, too played out for anything, from everything.

Left out, he might latch onto the wrong thing. Leaving himself out. Wrong things.

.   .   .

Water of life. That was his. When the company moved into bottled water, he was doing catalog copy for vitamin supplements. But it was he they brought up front. Nobody else. Liked what he had done. Put the ball in his court. Gave him free rein.

How was he to know? He had no duty, no obligation to know. He assumed they had people—whole staffs— scientists and lawyers to check things out.

Not pure.

Straight from the tap.

Well, who knew what it meant?

They walked from his brother's house, past dilapidated boxcars on the shunt, along the tracks. His brother handed him a beer, opened a package of cigarettes.

—Want a smoke?

—Sure.

He told a story.

His brother told a story.

It was the story of a guy older than them, a guy who wore glasses and played the clarinet and had a pensive look and a pensive mother.

They walked the tracks in the dying light.

After a while his brother got on things. The future. Wind power. Solar panels.

He took another cigarette. Another beer.

His brother got on these trains of the future. High speed. Run on electromagnetic lines. The electricity and magnets pulling people along from city to city, hub to hub, at safe, wonderful, awesome speeds.

But not even the speed of light.

Low Cover

Clump of rock.
Piece of metal.
In his side.
In his lung.

What he needed was a better diet. More exercise. Maybe stress reduction. He told himself not to worry. That was part of his problem, that tendency to worry.

He went in to see someone.

They cut his health insurance.

The lung had to come out.

All at once, Bill thought, the same fucking day.

Recovery took time; they really busted him up. When he was well enough to work, he had run through everything. The job was gone. Then the car. Then the house.

Miracle he survived, the doctor said.

Bill knew a flat piece of ground out by the dump. He made a little structure, warm and pretty dry, an old chair, food shelf. Not too bad. True, he could not walk very fast or exert himself for long. With one lung, what could anybody expect?

Kids went out to the dump.

To drink beer. Park.

He heard shots.

Sure, they came out to shoot their .22s. Shoot rats, cans, whatnot. Perfectly normal. They were kids.

· · ·

Bill had lost track. After he moved, some others, others before him, others after him, too, it seemed like everyone lost, lost out. He was not sure. Maybe it was not so bad, or maybe it was worse. Bill had no TV, no radio. No electricity. Newspaper, hell—there was plenty of newspaper blowing up from the landfill if he ever wanted to go catch a sheet.

The smoke had not always been there. It had started, Bill could not remember, was getting worse, though. He knew that. Seen the smoke when it was damn near nothing, a plume, maybe two wispy gray plumes, rising off the surface. Now it was a heavy fog, constant haze, no individual plumes unless you stirred some up digging. Bill thought that this was it: The smoke getting worse around the time they started digging.

Man came in a truck with a loudspeaker on the top. Had soft drinks and food, popcorn and hot dogs, music coming out of the loudspeaker.

Bill went down to the truck with some things in mind.

When everyone had a snack, man got out of the truck and talked through the loudspeaker. He talked about Economic Miracle.

We were first once—why not now?

Others have done it—why can't we?

Man went on at some length. Be hard, very hard, the first twenty years or so, but then all the boats would rise with the tide.

Bill and the others already salvaged cans. But with this new thing, there seemed no limit what could be sold— spent batteries, insecticide containers, industrial motor-cooling units.

Asbestos paid off.

Mercury was pure gold.

· · ·

Sometimes he felt like he was burning.

At night, Bill did it at night. Bill would have preferred to do it in the day, in the light, for all to see. But Bill knew he could not, not with one lung. He went to the school, broke a window, sloshed his gasoline, lit his rags.

He could not stay to watch his work.

There were limits to what he could do. The building was cinderblock. Carpeting, books, furniture, computers — all that would go.

If they built it back, he would burn it again.

The school was never rebuilt. The window frames were empty. The wind that blew through the building was scented with soot. Not even birds had taken roost in the burnt-out remains.

It had been a good morning, enough metal for some food and a bottle of wine. Bill had the bottle open, was nipping as he walked. He decided to go up close, peer in through the frame. Eyes were not what they had been. One of them he could hardly see out of anymore. Had to get his head right in there.

He could smell himself. Clothes, body, port on his breath. Stench and the bad eye and the wheezing lung and a limp, bit of a limp, something wrong with his knee. Worse when there were clouds. Bill could predict low cover with that knee.

Through the frame, dark and charred, he saw them, the kids covered with soot.

They started up and ran through the open doorway.

Bill stumbled back.

The kids got around him.

They ran in a circle.

He tried to get away. The circle moved with him.

—Teacher Bill, they said.

If they would leave him alone.

If they would let him go.

Bill could not think. Wine was spilling on the ground.

—Everything I said was wrong. Just lick their boots and hope to survive. That's all that matters.

Quicksilver glint of mercury, like the sun on arctic ice. Bill tried to pick it up. The arctic. That clean and frozen place, so far from the smoke and metal and the past, the wasted breath. If someone could crack that ice, what relic would be encased there?

Edge City

It was not a matter of liking it, of choice, of this or that, of "I want." More and more, he felt there was no choice. Especially in the morning, he felt this. Aside from the normal problems, the everyday problems like everyone else's everyday problems, he had some internal things, some personal problems. Or, really, character flaws.

His character was flawed, no doubt about it.

He felt bad about it, but what could he do?

Character flaw.

Last day, he was eating his lunch at his desk. Looking out at the stretch of tar- and gravel-covered roof, the distant trees, the sky. A plastic bag blew onto the roof. A heavy tan bag, woven plastic. Took a second to recognize it as a sandbag.

The first time was the worst. He had lost plenty of jobs, but that first time really knocked him on his ass. He'd send out two, three resumes a week for these jobs—great jobs that paid more than he had ever made and provided offices and health insurance and company cars—and he would sit in the house, drinking malt liquor, believing he was about to land the big one.

On the last day, when he was looking out the window, his supervisor told him it was all over.

He knew that.

—So what? he said.

—Don't get smart, the supervisor said.

—Smart?

—You aren't jack, the supervisor said. You aren't anything. You aren't fuck all.

He stood up. —I aren't what?

He needed any job, no matter how bad, to get a better job. It was like a test. A demonstration of how much shit one was willing to eat. He went to janitorial, security, telemarketing firms. He knew how to live cheap.

—You get two uniforms, the boss said.

—Okay.

—That's out of your first check.

—Okay.

—You break the baton, you pay for it.

—Okay.

—You want a big flashlight, that's your expense. And get some black shoes.

He was hoping for a place with closed-circuit TV in the lobby. Sit there and watch the screen.

They gave him a medical arts building downtown that dated from the turn of the century. Linoleum hallways lined with painted doors with frosted windows. The building stank of germicide and dental plaster. He had to walk all night, punch little wall-mounted machines to prove he made his rounds.

Seemed like he had been in this building when he was a child. The place had gone down since then. The remaining professionals were ancient or alcoholic or addicted, their shabby clients worse. Who, he wondered, would want teeth fabricated here?

Mostly vacant storefronts on the street level, but still a few going concerns—gutted-looking liquor store, barber shop, the House of Love.

House of Love in a storefront that had been a shoe repair and tobacco shop. Couple of female mannequins decked out in stockings and leather in the display window, with magazines, games, videos at their feet. The rest of the interior blocked with painted particle board. A sign advertising adult novelties.

He looked at the picture on a cassette box. He wondered what kind of business the place did days. It was always closed when he came on.

He had forgotten to change the timing belt at the recommended mileage, and it went out. Eight thousand after the recommendation.

—Forgot, his wife said. Jesus.

She was right. It was one of those mental things.

What could he do but fix the car, put it on the plastic?

Getting to be spring. His wife needed new clothes for spring. She got some. She got the clothes, and he had the car fixed, a brand new timing belt.

Best not to give it a thought.

Special deal. One time only. He could get a quilted nylon jacket with the security company's patch and an American flag on it for thirty-five bucks. Supplementary wear with the uniform. Order at work.

Some of the other guys, supervisors mostly, had the jacket. The jacket looked pretty good.

He turned his time card in at the main office every other Tuesday afternoon.

Ran into a guy there. A kid, really. The kid had a little scooter, like a moped, with a For Sale sign on it.

—What are you going to do next? his wife said. Read wrestling magazines?

—This will save me a fortune in gas, he said.

—It's not safe.

—It's fine.

—I hate it, she said.

—It's not like I'm asking you to ride it.

—You look like a clown, she said.

—This isn't my dream come true, he said, but we have got to downscale.

—We're still richer than the Chinese, he said. The Filipinos, the Indians. Hell, the Indians would kill to be in our shoes.

He should worry about looking stupid? He was just trying to somehow survive.

—None of this is my fault, he said.

He was not sure if this was true.

He pulled up to the curb, parked the bike, glanced at the House of Love.

One of the stockinged and gartered mannequins was holding a pair of handcuffs.

He did not have handcuffs. Not part of his equipment. Not, in fact, allowed.

He caught his reflection in the window: the thick body in the quilted nylon on the tiny moped.

Character flaw.

He always wanted to fly in a helicopter.

A NOTE ON THE TYPE

This book was set in a type face called Baskerville. The face is a facsimile reproduction of type cast from molds made for John Baskerville (1706–1775) from his designs. The punches for the revived Linotype Baskerville were cut under the supervision of the English printer George W. Jones. John Baskerville's original face was one of the forerunners of the type style known to printers as "modern face" — a "modern" of the period A.D. 1800.

Composed by ComCom,
a division of Haddon Craftsmen,
Allentown, Pennsylvania.

Printed and bound by
The Haddon Craftsmen, Scranton, Pennsylvania.